# INWARD BOUND

## RONIN MATTHEWS

ISBN: 978-1-923675-51-3 (Paperback)

NATIONAL LIBRARY OF AUSTRALIA

A catalogue record for this book is available from the National Library of Australia

Self-Published by Ronin Matthews with assistance by Clark & Mackay
Proudly printed in Australia by Clark & Mackay

# ABOUT THE AUTHOR

**RONIN MATTHEWS, AUTHOR** of *The Concrete Jungle*, has returned with another action-packed book in which people question the mind, body and spirit. Ronin was born in Nowra, New South Wales, Australia, and has worked in various jobs over his lifetime. Now he wants to share his love of writing with the world.

*All their life in this world and all their adventures had only been the cover of the title page: now, at last, they were beginning Chapter One of the Great Story, which no one on Earth has read, which goes on forever: in which every chapter is better than the one before.*

—C.S Lewis. 'The Last Battle',
the final book in *The Chronicles of Narnia*

# CHAPTER 1

## From the Concrete to the Desert

'JACOB! WAKE UP!' … Jaaaacob, wake up! … Jacob! Your mission is not done yet!'

That voice, that echoing voice, sounded like my mother's voice ringing in my ear. *Aaagh!*

As I took in a breath of radiated oxygen, the helicopter' seatbelt suspended me upside down. Gasping for air, my heart was pounding in my chest. The  was coursing through my body and I felt like I had just drunk five cups of coffee. Wait, what was going on? Was I in Heaven or Hell? But I couldn't see any angels or demons. Then it dawned on me, *Oh my goodness, I am alive! I am still alive.*

This was a miracle. I took a few minutes to enjoy it, but a wave of depression overcame me; I had survived the crash, but to no avail, as looking out, it was apparent I was in the Wasteland where there was no visible life whatsoever – just vase empty planes. *Great! But hang on! How on earth did I survive?*

Then my memory started to return. Of course … I got into a fistfight with John up above the city as he tried to escape in a helicopter. The iron dome defence system missile shot our helicopter out of the town into the Wasteland. Realising the severity of this issue, I just pulled out a cigarette from my back pocket, lit it with my lighter and laid upside down, waiting for the radiation to kill me. What was the point in even trying anymore? Life sucks, and I guess this is how I die, alone and miserable.

Just as I was about to indulge myself in the smoke from the cigarette, I heard a growl. I sighed heavily, contemplating whether it was worth escaping to find out what it was or just take the coward's way out and wait here to die. But, why not investigate?

I unbuckled my belt on the helicopter and I fell face first onto the helicopter floor. Luckily, I couldn't feel any pain due to the . After getting to my feet, I looked out at the green skies and the yellow sand of the Wastelands, and there I saw it. It was a figure in the distance, about a metre from the helicop-ter. I was confused. I mean, *who was that?* Out of confusion, I went to investigate; closer and closer I got to the figure, which looked familiar. I recognised the suit and the disfigured skin.

'John? John, is that you?' it look like John Spear, the Ceo of WeapCo  and the man I punched in the neck but it couldn't be it didn't look like him.

The figure stopped growling and looked up, but I could only see the back of the figure as it stood there in silence.

'John, is that you?'

The figure slowly started standing up straight. I was now scared as I didn't know how John would react. *Will he scream at me or kill me?* I didn't know how he was still alive, as I recalled I broke his windpipe.

'John?'

Suddenly, the figure sharply turned around to reveal John's body with his jaw hanging loose, his suit and skin covered in scars and sores, and his skin as white as a ghost. His eyes were glowing green from the .  His vocabulary was reduced to random grumbling and noises. But that made sense, as I had punched his vocal cord. Then, I could see his eyes staring at me like a rabid predator ready to catch its helpless prey.

'John!' I tried to appeal to the creature's humanity, if it even was, but to no avail, as John was no more; all that remained was an animal trapped in a man's body as it grumbled at me and began charging at me, rushing with its arms swinging around in circles and its bony feet rushing towards me at a surprisingly fast pace, considering the creature was half-dead.

As fast as I could, I started running back to the crashed helicopter, hoping to hide, or at least find a weapon to use against the creature. It began running on all fours like a dog, which only made it move even faster, and it was just grumbling all sorts of noises at me, yelling with its broken vocal cord. Some of the words resembled John's voice.

I finally reached the helicopter and looked around for something to use against the creature, but there was nothing, no weapons or loose objects, but before I could even reach the inside of the helicopter, The creature roared and leapt into the air, jumping so high that it blocked out the son. I closed my eyes as I waited for the beast to jump on top of me and eat me. I closed my eyes briefly. But still, nothing happened; *where was it?*

I opened my eyes and—nothing, it  had disappeared. Curious, I emerged from under the helicopter and looked around. There was only empty planes. The creature had vanished into thin air, or was he a part of my imagination? The radiation must be rotting away my brain.

'See you in the forest.'

I turned around sharply; it was John's voice, yet I couldn't see him anywhere. *Where was that coming from? Okay, the radiation was definitely rotting away my brain.*

I could do nothing about it; this was all getting too much to deal with, and I needed to rest. So, I sat down near the broken helicopter to relax and escape the scorching heat, as the sun had burned my skin to the point that I could feel myself turning red.

*What am I supposed to do now?* I had no plan in mind and, honestly, no will to live. If it wasn't for that stupid chemical cocktail, I wouldn't have to worry about this whole situation because the crash in the helicopter, for a normal human being, would have killed them, not to mention the level of radiation in this place, which would have burnt their skin. This was happening right now and was the worse pain I had ever experienced. *Augh!* I may as well walk into the barren Wasteland and find a sand dune to die in.

I got up and began death marching into the desert as the helicopter disappeared out of the corner of my eye. All I could see was sand upon more sand and a vast horizon stretching forever.

Thanks to the  coursing through my body, my cells were repairing at a rapid rate. However, it was complete agony as the radiation was burning away my skin every second while the healing factor was helping it grow back. Imagine having your skin around your entire body peeled off, only for it to return and start the whole process over and over. My eyes were barely able to stay open, as the sand, wind and radiation kept burning my eyes.

I didn't know how long I could keep this up as the  in my body was starting to wear off, and in about four hours, I would be dead meat. I didn't know where I was going; the whole effort to stay alive seemed futile. I finally gave up and collapsed onto the desert sand, weak and broken; my body was in an immense amount of pain, my skin was burning, and I was no longer able to cope. I crouched on my knees looking up into the green sky with tears rolling down my face; I knew I was going to die, but now the realisation was starting to hit me. What would be my legacy for my 27 years on Earth?  A nobody who lost everything – my family, my home, my love. I was a shell of a broken man reduced to nothing and condemned to die an agonising death as I screamed out from both the physical and emotional pain. *God, why have you done this? Why have you done this to me! WHY!*

With no strength left, I curled up on the desert in a foetal position. Ready for the end, I suddenly heard a noise!

*Great!* Now my body was going to be eaten by some radiated creature or some zombie or whatever this hellhole produced. But no, it sounded like a machine. Getting to my feet with renewed strength, I looked into the distance – it was a truck! I stood waving my arms like I had bugs in them, completely ignoring the pain from my burning skin. The truck stopped and started heading towards me. I couldn't believe it; I was undoubtedly saved. But as the truck began to appear, my vision began to blur. The last thing I saw was a figure in a radiation suit staring down at me before I collapsed into unconsciousness.

# CHAPTER 2

**MY EYES FLICKERED** and then widened. I was lying in a hospital bed with a hospital gown on and a hospital band around my arm. *Where the hell was I?*

I looked up and saw an African-American doctor wearing a white doctor's coat and looking at a clipboard. I could hear a familiar voice in the background; 'Ella!', But how she was back in America, hopefully safe and sound, but another voice came through my ear.

'Doctor, the patient is still in a comatose state.'

The doctor looked up from his charts. 'Very well, nurse, inform me of the patient's condition'.

My eyes shot open, and I was back in the real world. The Wastelands night sky was lit up with a dark reddish-black as I peered through the reinforced windscreen. I was in the passenger seat of a heavy, rigid, rad-proof truck with the only light source being the white light from the overhead light. I looked around the truck and noticed a slightly overweight, middle-aged man with an overgrown beard and a dragon tattoo on his forearm. He was dressed in foreman gear and wearing sunglasses. The driver looked over at me and said, 'Well, good morning, sleepy head.'

Confused as to who this person was, I mumbled, 'Ahh … good morning.'

'I saw you lying in that desert and thought I had to pick you up. Man, it was a miracle I found you. What the hell are you doing all the way out here?'

All I could do was rub my eyes and try to wake myself up. 'Oh, it's a long story'.

The truck driver smiled and let out a small laugh. 'To be out here without rad gear is either remarkable or stupid or maybe a bit of both. He looked at me and then back out the windscreen, concentrating on driving. 'My name is Marc, by the way'.

I pulled myself up, chucked on a seatbelt and stared directly at the truck driver. I was still unsure about this person, but nonetheless, he'd saved me, so I should be polite. I stretched out my hand. 'Jacob! Thanks for picking me up!'

Marc nodded slightly and withheld his hand.

I put my hand down, looking quite foolish. 'So, where are you heading?'

'Depends—are you heading to American Division City?'

'American Division City!' I let out a chuckle.

'I am from there, but I'm making a delivery to Asian Division City. After I'm done there, I can drop you back home for a small fee.'

'Umm, yer … thanks.' I didn't have any money, but I would figure something out when we got back home.

'So, Marc, are you with the military?'

Marc smiled. 'Me? No, not for a long time. I am a Global truck driver.'

That made sense to me now as to why he was this far out in the Wastelands. Global truck driving was one of the most dangerous jobs on the planet. They delivered cargo between all the major cities on Earth, which meant travelling through the Wastelands. The job was high-paying, but the fatality rate was high, as many drivers lose their lives to pirates and crashes, and some get stuck in the Wastelands and die of radiation poisoning. It took a different breed to do this type of job. Mostly alcoholics, drug addicts, adrenaline junkies, and downright crazy people did this kind of work

Marc spat out the window. 'So, you still haven't explained what you are doing out here?'

Having marched out through the desert and having the radiation burn my skin repeatedly, I didn't feel like talking to Marc right now. 'Look, I really don't want to talk about it!'

Marc just concentrated on driving. 'Not a big talker, are you?'

I had nothing to say to that, just focusing on the planes ahead, asking myself the same questions over and over: 'How come I didn't die? What purpose could I possibly serve on this planet?' I'm a nobody with no real skills except knowing how to kill people, and everyone in my life has either died or left-me. But I honestly ignored those questions as I guess the survivor's guilt was kicking in; I really could do with some alcohol right now.

The truck was enjoyable because it was sealed and lined with lead to withstand the full radioactive fallout. However, the truck was able to filter out any radiation that might infiltrate every hour using a powerful spray that blasted us in our faces. Marc and I looked up at the ceiling as a speaker screamed out, *clarification beginning*, then we were blasted straight in the face. Marc and I laughed afterwards. 'Man, those sprays are annoying as all hell,' I yelled out.

Marc looked over at me, possibly noticing that I wasn't looking the best. 'Hey mate, are you feeling alright?'

My face had turned white, and my veins and eyes burned green. My body felt like I was about to throw up! My time was up as the in my body was breaking down thanks to my metabolism, and I was suffering from severe withdrawal. 'Marc, is there anything I can throw up in?'

Marc looked at me with a shocked expression as if he had never seen anyone look like that before. 'Not in this truck!' He handed me an empty ration package. 'Here, do it in this!'

I threw up my entire guts in the bag, and I was feeling a bit crazy as the whole room began to spin, then *bang!* I hit my head on the truck dashboard.

I was beginning to slip back into sleep, which meant they came out: 'I love you, hunny'. 'Jacob, I am sorry'. 'Jacob, I need to do this'. *Jacob!* Every time I close my eyes, I hear them and see them – the memories, the phantoms of a dreadful and painful past, reminders of what had been and what could have been; every time I replay them in my mind, it hurts. I see and hear visions of Ella lying on the floor covered in her own blood; Yendan dying in the hospital bed; and my mother bruised. The many horrors from the PTSD as a result of when I was a formal soldier and a soldier of the streets. But I didn't know what was worse, the actual events themselves or the constant screams I hear daily. Now I understand why people fear the dark. My eyes began to slowly open and I could see the pitch-black screen out ahead, but I was in a sort of tired trans-state as my body fell asleep. Yet, my brain was so overstimulated that the neurons in my head overwhelmed my eyes to the point that they burned through my socket.

'You alright?'

I looked over to find Marc's face concerned at my state. I bet he had second thoughts about letting me onto his truck. As I made one last cough, vomit landed into the ration pack. 'Fine, thanks for asking'. I wasn't okay as I was half-dead, but no point telling him that. 'So, how long until we reach Asian Division City?'

'Five days away.'

'Five days! I must get to American Division City as soon as possible.'

'Calm your farm; we will get there like I said. We have to make a delivery. Drop off this cargo at Asian Division City, and then I will drop you off—'

*Bang!* Marc and I looked at each other as I yelled, 'What was that?!'

Marc scrambled around in a panic. 'Look out!'

The truck came to a complete stop as Marc slammed the breaks on, and the tyres skidded through the sand. In front of us was an old rad-proof truck, probably from a Global truck driver who died out here in the Wastelands. Marc looked at the ruined, corroded truck and noticed the skeleton sitting in the front seat.

'Looks recent ... at least an hour dead. The poor bastard must have run out of power,' said Marc.

'Yes, the truck is lead-line, that's only one part. Specific mechanisms in the car allow it to function in the Wastelands without damaging it. Without power sustaining the truck, it will quickly deteriorate from the large amount of radiation in the Wastelands. I only know this because, in the military, they had trucks that were more advanced than this, but the basics were the same.'

Marc looked down at his steering wheel.

'What a terrible way to go out. You know that person?'

Marc sighed. 'No, but it's still a scary thought ... you know, the realities of the Wastelands. Ahh... all we are trying to do is make an honest day living.'

'You know there are easier ways to make money, right? Why do you do this job?'

Marc looked over at me. 'Mate, do you know how hard it is to find work without a fancy college degree and a formal education? I mean, I barely know any algebra, and I am illiterate; this is the only type of job I can do.'

I nodded in sympathy. I knew what it was like as I had nothing handed to me. Marc sighed and said, 'Poor guy,' bowing his head in silence out of respect for the dead person. Usually, I would be more sympathetic, but after what I'd been through, I didn't give a damn about some dead body and only wanted to get home.

'Okay, come on Marc, I feel for him too, but life goes on; let's get to where we were going.'

Marc nodded. 'Yer let's!'

But we both heard that banging noise again. 'Wait a moment, do you notice something?' I looked at Marc as he turned his truck around. The destroyed truck had red graffiti on it: *Bullseye!* I looked at it in shock. But who wrote it? Suddenly, a bullet hit Marc's truck's windscreen; luckily, it was reinforced glass, so the bullet only dinted the glass. But in the distance, I saw them, or at least their eyes. Up in the sand dunes ahead I could see the purple reflection of their eyes, and by the looks, there were many of them.

'Marc, we need to get out of here now!'

There was a tap on the driver's side window. A figure dressed in a green hazmat suit and wearing old military-grade night vision goggles, stared at us with his purple eyes. 'Open up this truck, or we will break it open!'

I couldn't tell the figure's gender as the voice was obscured under the mask. Mark and I were both concerned. The truck was rad-sealed and if we opened it, we'd both die.

Marc sighed, 'Blast! They must be pirates.'

'Damn, Marc! Quick, floor it! Floor it now!'

But before Mark could answer, the mysterious figure knocked on the glass and yelled, 'Open up the back, or we will blast our way in!'

I turned to Mark. 'Do we have any weapons in this vehicle?'

'Only in the back cargo hold, but they are sealed up, and by the time we get to them, the pirates would have gotten to them.'

'Okay, are there any auto-turrets or protection capabilities?'

'No! International law forbids trucks like this carrying weapons unless sealed-up cargo.'

'Really? International law still exists? Anyway, there is no time to think of that now. Floor it!'

Marc nodded, and he hit the electric peddle. But the truck got bogged in the sand just as the figure pulled his rifle that he was nursing in his arm and began shooting at the driv-er's side window was hit from a red plasma bolt shattering the window. A metal shutter shot up and sealed the window, which was a secondary measure to protect the truck from possible contamination. 'Floor it, Marc! One more shot, and we are toast!'

The truck pulled back in time, and shot backwards, like a bullet travelling so fast that the truck in front of us was quickly disappearing before our very eyes. But we could still see the red laser bolts flying through the air; luckily, they all missed our truck.

Marc screamed out in pain. 'Oh no, oh no, no, no!'

I flinched in pain, *agggh!* I turned around to find a pirate holding a laser pistol and pointing it directly through a win-dow from the door that leads to the cargo hold. Just as the pirate was about to fire another shot, another shutter shot down which sealed us off, so he couldn't get in. Plus, the door locks from our side, and there was no way we would let him in. But I wasn't worrying about that now, as Marc looked pretty bad. A bullet had pierced through his chest, leaving a medi-um-sized hole. He was struggling for air.

'Jacob! Do you know how to drive a truck?'

'Are you kidding?'

'Do you know how to drive?'

'*Ugh!* Well, I can give it a try.'

'Fine, you're going to have to take the wheel.'

I don't know why I must always be caught in these situations. But anyway, I was here now and needed to snap out of it. A red laser flew at our truck and hit the driver's side mirror, taking it out completely.

'Okay Marc, we better hurry up!' Marc and I, without thinking, quickly manoeuvred over each other, swapping seats, and with the full might of my foot, I floored it! The wheels on the truck spun so fast that they were shooting sand all over the desert. The truck shot off into the darkness of the night.

I had no idea where we were going. Still, all I knew was I had an injured truck driver in the passenger seat and very few resources for us to survive in the Wastelands.

Mark began breathing heavily and yelling as blood came pouring out his mouth.

'Marc, come on mate, stay with me!'

Soon the truck was far enough away that the enemies couldn't catch us.

'It hurts ... it hurts so much.'

'Stay with me, Mark. Is there a first-aid kit in this truck?'

'In the back ...'

I removed my seatbelt and grabbed the outdated white box with a red cross on the front; it looked like this thing hadn't been updated in years. Nonetheless, it would have to do. I opened it, knowing that it would be a waste of time – but there was hope after all, as I pulled out a long silver device called a medical sealant tool. The device shot out purple gel into Marc's blast wound. The liquid quickly solidified and closed the wound as Marc's heart rate slowed.

'Thanks, kid! Thanks for having my back. I would be lost without you.' His breathing returned to normal, and he was calmer.

'No problem. Couldn't let my only truck driver die on me now, can I?'

'Haha, yeah … but I could really go for a drink right now, and I mean the tough stuff.'

While the wound was sealed up, Marc was still looking quite pale and weak. He could barely move.

'Do you want some water?'

'Water? I haven't touched that stuff in years – surprised that my kidneys lasted this long.'

'Sorry, kid, we will just have to camp out here if you don't mind. I don't feel up to driving right now.'

'Alright …'  I had to admit I was a bit tired myself as Mark stood up and clicked a switch above him, sending the cabin of the truck into low power mode as the lights all went out and left only the necessary survival gear on, which included some purple lighting.

Marc and I looked up at the windscreen into the darkness, hoping to eventually get some rest, but one of the good things was that now, with only a small amount of lighting, we could both finally see the stars.

'Oh my …' I murmured.

The shining heaven of stars only complemented the full moon, which lit the night with a bright glow. The night sky was filled with constellations of all shapes and sizes. It was a sight I hadn't seen in a long time. I even saw a meteor shooting through the sky and disappearing again. I was absolutely amazed; I hadn't seen the stars in years, as light pollution plagued the skies of American Division City. The glass dome hindered the vision of the stars, so it was too blurry to see them, even if we could. Yet in all their majesty, they were a free gift from God. Looking at the stars gave me renewed hope that I wasn't alone; there was a big universe out there that I had yet to explore.

However, Marc wasn't in a talking mood, until out of nowhere, 'So kid, do you have a special lady waiting for you back home?'

'I did. My saint of a mother and somewhat girlfriend awaits me back home.'

'Somewhat?'

I sighed. 'It's complicated. I miss them every day.'

'It's funny ... it feels like yesterday that I was sitting down eating chips as we rebuilt our home – and now it feels like they are a million miles away ... may as well be on a different planet.'

'What about you, mate? Have you got a lucky someone waiting for you at home?'

'Yer ... I have a wife and a daughter.'

'Really? What's their names?'

'Lacy and Jordan.'

'Congratulations! How long have you two been married?'

'Going on ten years now, and our daughter just turned six.'

'You're a fortunate man.'

'Hardly, my wife actually filed for divorce a month ago.'

'Yer, it's hard for a marriage to survive when I am gone for months. But I missed them so much!' Mark stared out the window as a tear fell down his face. 'I missed so much of their life ... my daughter's birth, her first words ... I missed so much of her life because I was out on the open road. Not thinking of the time wasted as slowly my life began to fall apart. It's funny ... when I was younger, all I could think about was work-ing non-stop to provide for them, so I worked my fingers to the bone to make ends meet, and now that I am older, I real-ise they were years wasted that I could have spent with my daughter. I have run out of time; I love them so much.'

'Don't worry, Marc. Before you know it, you will have them in your arms.'

'I would love that, Jacob. I would love that more than anything in the world.'

'Believe me, Marc, I have made mistakes and ruined many relationships that I wish I could take back.'

'Ha! A young man like you has all the time in the world. Not like this old fossil.'

'But so do you.'

Marc didn't say anything for a while as he looked down at his feet. 'We will rest up and continue our journey in the morning.'

'Are you sure the pirates won't find us out here?'

'Positive! We shot out of there quickly, and it didn't look like they had reliable transport, so I am pretty sure we are safe.'

I fell back into the seat, relaxing, waiting for my heart rate to drop. Finally, I sat forward and said, 'Wait, what about the pirate in the back?'

Marc leaned over and clicked a button. 'Done!'

'What's done?'

'The pirate's gone!'

'How do you know?'

'I diverted all oxygen from the cargo hold back to the cockpit.'

I looked at him, shocked that Marc could do that. 'Are you sure we are safe?' But as I looked at Marc, I noticed he wasn't looking so good. 'Hey Marc, are you doing alright?'

Marc just gave a small laugh. 'Sure, kid, never better. I'm fine.'

'You don't look fine. Is there anything—'

'I said I'm fine!' His face reddened and his voice increased in tone.

I stopped at that point.

'Sorry, kid, this job takes a toll on you over time. Plus, forgive me, but I did have a laser bolt shoot through my chest.'

'That's okay, I know what that's like, I have been shot at many times. The fear of what awaits you on the other side and the fear of never seeing the ones you love again is a scary thought.'

'Quite the soldier, aren't you!'

'I know, right? I have been in so many battles that I have lost count, and I have lost so many people in my lifetime that I could fill a swimming pool.' I stopped to contemplate what I had been through. 'You know, Marc, out of my entire group, I was the only one to survive; it is tough.' I sat back in my chair. 'Sometimes I just don't know what God sees in me; I mean, why me? Why was I the only one to survive? But you know what the scariest thought is, Marc?'

'What?'

'When was my luck going to run out? That's the real question that scares me the most.'

Marc was about to speak when the weather changed dramatically. We both looked through the windscreen as an acid rainstorm came in and began belting down dark-green, highly acidic raindrops on the truck, but at least the rain was peaceful.

'There was no point driving in this weather; we will just have to wait it out.'

*Knock! Knock!* We both jumped. 'What was that?' I called out.

'Probably just sand winds blowing on the side of the truck.'

If only that was the case; while it made logical sense, my gut told me something was about to happen.

*Knock! Knock!* Marc looked over at the driver's side mirror, and by the look on his face, he saw something that scared the daylights out of him.

'Marc, what's wrong?'

'Jacob, there is someone out there!'

At that moment, my instincts reached down for the handgun in the coffee holder while looking through the window. But I couldn't see anything, the wind and rain making the visibility outside impossible. 'Marc, I can't see anything.'

Marc continued to look out; there was nothing but silence. 'Guess I was—'

*Bang!* The sealed-up window on the cargo-hold door came down as a figure wearing a hazmat suit stood before them. The pirate must have survived.

Before I could grab the gun, Marc reached down and pulled out the handgun, pointing it directly at the figure. A calibre bullet went flying towards the figure, but luckily for the figure, it went back into the cargo hold.

'Marc, can we get into the back?'

'No, there is no oxygen back there. If you go back there without a hazmat suit on, you will die.'

'Can you return oxygen back there?'

'Unfortunately, no, I needed to replenish the oxygen after our windows were broken, which would mean taking oxygen from the cabin.'

'Blast! So, what do we do?'

'Nothing. We can't just fire aimlessly into the cargo hold because you might hit a fuel canister or something back there.'

'Marc, get us out of here!'

'Agreed,' Marc reached for the wheel and turned on the engine. But we were too late. We heard a noise from the back of the truck, and the back sliding door shot up. We heard multiple footsteps entering the truck.

'Oh no! They managed to access the cargo bay. They could take our cargo!'

I took off my seatbelt and peered through the cargo door. While I couldn't see anything, as there was barely any lighting, I could hear running around in the back; they ran so fast that they looked like shadows. I was scared as I didn't know what they would do with us. There was no escape as none of us could survive the Wastelands. Suddenly, two astronaut-like figures appeared at the cargo-door window and in front of the windscreen, which caused both of us to jump out of our seats.

'Marc, who are they?'

'I am guessing more pirates? The friend out the back must have called for reinforcements.'

The figure near the cargo door window stepped back and disappeared as the figure in front of us remained. There was silence as no one said anything, and then a canister landed on Marc's lap.

Neothyl began filling the truck and we started to feel dizzy. We began coughing up all over the floor then slipped into unconsciousness. After about two minutes, we collapsed in our seats

# CHAPTER 3

**WHEN I WOKE** up, my burning lungs tried gasping for air with every breath feeling like agony. The anaesthetic finally wore off, and I was once again conscious. I was now in the cargo bay with an oxygen mask on; at least the pirates had the decency to give us oxygen masks while they kidnapped us. But I was also tied to the wall of the truck with zip ties. Marc was lying beside me, snoring his head off, sounding as if he had a frog in his throat. I tried wiggling around, hoping to get free, but no luck. Around us, cargo crates were piled neatly, with some unsealed as the pirates rummaged through them. Whatever was in these boxes must be worth a lot of money, or why would we have so many people coming after us?

I turned to Marc and shook him with my foot. 'Marc! Marc! Come on, wake up! Marc!'

He finally woke and looked around. 'Jacob, why are we in the cargo bay?'

'You tell me, mate. What is in those cargo crates?'

Marc shrugged. 'I don't know. I'm just a delivery driver. My job was to transfer this cargo to Asian Division City; it wasn't my job to know.' He paused as we heard the truck start up and we could feel the vibration on the tyres moving. 'Wait! Who the hell is driving my truck!'

I could tell that Marc was furious as his face went as red as a tomato.

'Whoever is touching my truck, I am going to kill personally; no one touches my pride and joy.'

Marc seemed scared at this point. I wasn't. I had been in this situation before, and honestly, it felt like another detour, which was annoying. I only wanted to get home, and now I was getting involved in more drama, which I didn't need. 'Marc, do you reckon they actually are pirates?'

'Maybe, but then again, out here, who knows what is kidnapping us. The Wastelands are a cesspool for all sorts out here.'

That didn't put my mind at ease, but there was no point sitting around. I looked for something sharp to get us out of there, but it was no good. There was nothing, so I moved to Plan B.

Luckily, the kidnappers weren't smart enough to tie us to the wall. Instead, they tied us to a pole attached to the wall. So, without thinking, I slid the zip tie to the sharpest corner and began sawing at the zip tie to get free. With a lot of grunting and pulling, I managed to get free.

Marc cheered. 'Great! Now, can you get me free?'

'Is there an easier way to get you free, Marc?'

'Over in the far corner is a Stanley knife.'

Finally, we were free — but I spoke too soon, as in the corner, standing near the cargo door, was one of the green figures holding a military-issue plasma pistol, designed like a Glock-13 but capable of shooting plasma bolts. In an unknown language, it screamed at us. We held our hands up as the truck stopped.

The truck door began opening as the metal shutter shot open, and within a second, light pierced through the darkness of the cargo hold; we were clearly not in the Wastelands anymore. The truck must have docked in an enclosed environment.

The doors opened, and another figure in a green radiation suit with purple eyes entered the cargo hold, but what was surprising was it didn't have any weapons on it whatsoever; it just looked at Marc and me as the other figure stood there pointing its gun at us.

'Quick, Marc,' I whispered, 'zigzag … take out the first figure while I take out the second figure.'

Marc nodded, and rushed towards the first figure, grabbing him by the torso. We were both unarmed, so we had to move quickly. Marc zigzagged as the figure shot a blast, which missed my head by a millimetre. I tackled the unarmed figure, trying to take it down. But the first figure pistol-whipped Marc to the floor as he shot back, holding his now-bleeding mouth. My takedown of the second figure failed as the figure got the upper hand and threw me down to the truck floor. The two of us got to our knees with both hands behind our backs as the second astronaut-looking figure got up off the floor. Coughing sounds could be heard from under the mask. The first figure then stood in front of us. She removed her helmet and revealed a beautiful Middle Eastern woman with tanned skin, black hair, and brown eyes – nothing like I had expected.

After capturing us and forcing us to the ground, the mysterious woman turned to the other figures pointing a gun towards us as a third figure walked up the truck ramp and stood near the Middle Eastern woman. The two of them began speaking Arabic. We both had no idea what they were saying. I had never been deployed to the Middle East, so I had no idea what they were saying.

After finishing their conversation, the third figure walked behind us. As the second figure followed her, the third figure pulled out a sidearm. I could hear the gun being pulled out of the holster, and the two of them pointed their guns at our backs and began escorting us off the truck.

We were in a small, enclosed village with its own artificial dome around it, which looked like it had seen better days. The spaced-out buildings were shaped in the style of traditional mud houses; the tallest buildings were only two storeys high. The three figures began leading us into one of the buildings. Marc and I were completely afraid because it was uncharted territory even for me. We didn't know what was in this building and what precisely this village was. I didn't realise there were settlements outside of the cities as I didn't think life would be able to sustain itself out of the town. But I guess I was wrong. The figures, with their guns pointed at our backs, began leading us into their house, possibly as hostages. I still didn't know why we were still alive, but we will soon find out.

Entering the house, The figures jabbed Marc and me in the back with their guns, and one of them spoke in plain English: 'Sit!'

Not wanting to argue with them, we both crouched on the ground in a monk position, waiting to see what may occur next. Two of the figures walked in front of us and began removing their masks and goggles. The first figure was a Middle Eastern woman in her late-50s with grey hair and blue eyes. The second one was a Middle Eastern girl who looked around fourteen years of age. She was smaller than the other two figures with brown hair and brown eyes.

'Marc, are they going to kill us?'

'I don't know, but I am not liking this situation at all.'

The two women stood in front of us, not saying a word, holding their rifles in their hands. They looked scared, as if they didn't know what to do with us. They chatted to each other back and forth in Arabic.

Suddenly, the conversation between the two women stopped as the third woman entered the building, shooting Marc and me a  threating look. We both quickly broke eye contact with her so as not to get ourselves killed. She walked from the doorway into the living room and continued the conversation with her family in Arabic. They started setting up multiple dishes around a rug and began preparing dinner for themselves, treating us like we were never here.

I couldn't wait any longer; I had to think of something quick! I hit Marc with my leg to get him up. 'Marc, you see the door?'

'Yer!'

'Head toward it and get help.'

He nodded and proceeded to get to his feet, then slowly tiptoed to the door. Making sure not to make a sound, Marc had the misfortune of accidentally hitting the wooden door with his foot, which caused him to stumble back in pain while holding his foot. I was hoping they didn't hear that, but they would have to be deaf. The three women turned to us, and the youngest shouted, 'Sit down!'

I didn't know why, but the commanding nature of the women compelled me to sit down.

We could have made a runner, but they probably would have shot us before we walked out the door as they had their rifles close to them. The only option was to fight the three women, which meant waiting when their guard was down.

'Come,' ordered the older woman, gesturing to us, 'take a seat over here!'

A shiver ran down my spine and an unease settled in my stomach. 'Are you going to kill us?'

'Not if the two of you come and join us.'

We both could see no other option; not wanting to argue with the ladies, we sat down around the mat in a circle, joining them as the youngest plated us up with multiple exotic dishes. The food looked mouth-watering to me, but Mark didn't share in my excitement; judging by his face, he was ready to throw up.

This whole encounter was strange. Our captors kept talking to themselves in Arabic and completely ignored us. We sat there confused until the women finally showed us some attention; the youngest finally spoke up in English: 'Eat! You boys need your strength.'

We were too scared to eat, as we didn't know the catch.

'What's wrong with it?' I asked.

The women stopped talking, shot each other a look, smirked, then burst out laughing. The older woman replied, 'Nothing is wrong with it; please eat.'

Marc and I didn't say a word as we both picked up our plates, staring at each other to see which one of us would be brave enough to eat the food, but the younger woman then lost her patience and at the top of her lungs, screamed, 'Eat!'

An awkward silence soon followed as the women began laughing and talking to themselves while we ate our food in silence.

'So, what are you going to do with us?'

The women stopped and began facing us as Marc stood there in shock.

The girl asked us, 'How are you enjoying your meal?'

At that moment, my nerves got the better of me as I had lost patience. 'Enough playing games! Tell us who you are? Where are we? And what do you plan to do with our truck and cargo?'

Then, out of fear, silence descended; the women looked scared and surprised.

The older woman asked, 'You two are not from around here, are you?'

'How did you figure that out?' I replied sarcastically.

The lovely young Arabic woman spoke first. 'Well, for starters, not one of you asked to join us, and not one of you has touched your food.'

Marc and I slowly reached for our bowls and began eating the food.

Marc mumbled, 'Thank you for the food.'

The three women gradually relaxed and finally began showing us some attention:

'So, where are you lovely people from?'

'We both originated from American Division City?'

They all nodded and the young woman asked, 'Aww, you Americans?'

'Yer, I guess you can say that? Who are you people? And where are we?' I probed.

She laughed. 'Of course, how rude of me … my name is Ashilya, and this is my mother, Sara, and my younger sister, Yasmin.'

Yasmin greeted us with a high-pitched 'hello', waving to us.

'Lovely to meet you, ladies – now, can you tell us where we are?'

Marc had lost his patience. 'Screw that, ask them in their gobbledygook language where the hell my truck is!'

'We can all speak English, asshole!' Yasmin snapped.

'Easy, sis! They are scared,' hissed Ashilya. 'Your truck is fine, but the cargo, on the other hand, we need it!'

Marc snapped, 'For what! Where exactly are we?'

'In Afghanistan!'

Marc and I yelled out, 'Afghanistan!' we were both passed out at the time and being out back in the cargo we had no idea we were heading to Afghanistan.

Suddenly, Sara signalled to us to be quiet and  held a single finger to her mouth. Then, we could hear the sound of truck tyres pulling up near the building as high beams reflected through the window. Whatever was out there made the girls uneasy.

'Is it them?' asked .

'I don't know, . Quick! Yasmin, get the lights.' Sara turned to us. 'You boys, get down!'

Not knowing what was happening, Marc and I dropped down as Yasmin rushed over to the light switch and turned off the lights, leaving the room in darkness. Suddenly, a white light beam flew past the window. The light was different to the high beam of a truck as it clearly resembled the beam of a searchlight. Luckily, the light disappeared as fast as a phantom, and the room descended into darkness again.

Marc and I were as confused as ever as we shot each other weird looks. There was an awkward silence until Sara peered through the curtain. 'All clear!'

Marc was about to turn the lights on when Yasmin snapped at him, 'Are you crazy! Don't turn on the lights!'

'Why, what's going on?'

'That was a patrol. I guess the curfew is now in effect.'

'Curfew! Why do you have a curfew?' demanded Marc

Sara explained, 'The Afghanistan regime has implemented a curfew from seven pm to six am.'

Now I had lost my patience. 'Okay, we are still confused as hell as to what's happening.'

'Boys, take a seat, and we will explain everything,' chided Sara.

We gathered around, waiting for the women to explain what was happening.

# CHAPTER 4

'**YOU RECKON THEY** will be back?' Yasmin asked her mother.

'Let's hope not, Yasmin. Come and sit down; we may as well enjoy our dinner. So, boys, it's time to catch you up. How well do you know your history?'

Marc and I just looked at each other; neither of us barely finished school, let alone paid attention in history class. I answered, 'Umm, we are a little rusty. You might need to catch us up.'

Marc echoed, 'Yeah, like Jacob said, you may need to catch us up.'

Sara just sighed and rolled her eyes. 'Alright, so here is what happened, as I know for a fact that ancienthistory isn't really popular subject in the age of computers and technology: After the old empire, United States of America withdrew from Afghanistan, Afghanistan fell back into Taliban rule. At that point, Afghanistan was considered a weak nation. But that all changed once Israel declared war on Palestine! After that, the dynamic of the Middle East changed. Palestine fell, then Israel, then Egypt, then Qatar. After the fall of the United States of America, the European Union declared war on Iran,

UAE and Saudi Arabia, and just like that, the Middle East went up in flames; the situation only worsened as oilfields began to dry up; nation after nation fell, all trying to salvage what little oil the Middle East had left. Many nations fell as the region went up in flames, leaving only one nation to survive: Afghanistan!

'The Taliban survived like cockroaches and quickly annexed regions of the Middle East from Pakistan to Turkey under the brutal dictatorship of the Afghanistan regime! This town is just a fraction of the villages that are all spread out across the Wastelands, all ruled under individual, Taliban-appointed governments, with each sphere holding its own military and police force that governs Afghan law.'

sighed. 'For years, our sisters had remained hidden like shadows, avoiding the patrols, because if the Taliban finds out that we are husbandless, there is no telling what they would do with us.'

'Okay, I understand all that, but I have one question for you.' Mark held his right hand in the air. 'Why the hell did you steal my truck? How did you even manage to steal my truck and go unnoticed?'

Meanwhile, my eyes were focusing on something completely different. There was a glare coming from the crack in the floorboard. 'What's that?'

Sara explained, 'Our resistance movement received outside intel from an unknown source alerting us of a cargo truck driving through the Wastelands with weapons that would aid our movement. It was hard, but thanks to the countless sacrifices of many brave soldiers, resistance members managed to steal suits and a rover that was housed in a military warehouse and capture the truck. Unfortunately, the Taliban managed to capture the truck.'

'For now!' Yasmin cut in. 'But we intend to get it all back.'

I was blown away at how organised these women were.

'Hold up, you mentioned a resistance movement. What is that?' I was confused as I wasn't aware of any movement.

'We are part of an independent resistance movement built from multiple villages around the Middle East with some backing from outside sources that are trying to overturn Taliban rule. Our mission is to provide freedom and prosperity to our villages and to all villages; to have the same rights as any other individual in other cities. But we can—'

Marc was getting increasingly agitated. 'Oh enough of this rubbish! Tell me where—'

'Marc! Stop!'

'No, Jacob! I want my truck back.'

'Marc, wait!'

'What?!'

I stood up, looked at the loose floorboards and with brute strength I kicked in the floorboards to reveal a concealed weapons crate, which contained four A100 laser rifles.

'Give me!' Marc rushed over and quickly picked up an A100 rifle, released the safety mechanism and pointed it directly at the three women, who all stood up with their hands in the air. I stepped back in shock.

'Tell us where the exact location of my truck is, or I will start shooting.'

'Wait, wait!' Sara stood there with tears rolling down her eyes out of the fear of losing her daughters. 'Your truck is on the other side of town in the hangar. If you let us go, we will take you there.'

'Jacob, what do you think?'

'I think we should trust them.'

Marc sighed again and threw down the rifle. 'My truck and my cargo better be intact!'

The women nodded as Sara said, 'I promise your truck will be fine.'

'Alright, take us to our truck.'

'We can't ... we will have to wait for tomorrow. It is getting too bright; the Taliban will see us. We will have to wait for dusk; until then, you too are more than welcome to stay here. ! Yasmin! Prepare a bed for these two fellows!'

The two girls rushed to the nearest closet and pulled out some blankets and pillows.

Marc shook his head. 'How do we know you won't kill us?'

'You have our word. We will not hurt you! We need each other, as having two men like you will come in handy. Now get some rest!'

I knew it was stupid to sleep as they may kill us in our sleep. But I will give them the benefit of the doubt as, by the sound of things, they needed us alive. Plus, I was tired, and Mark was feeling the same by the look of him. After my head hit the pillow, I was out like a light.

I hated sleep; for me, sleep is when the demons come out. I used to numb it with alcohol, but this time I would have to face them head-on. What was it going to be this time? A beach? The little girl? The battle with the Kangasharks?

'Hey!'

I opened my eyes to find , dressed in night garments, standing over me and looking concerned. 'Are you alright?'

'I am fine, what makes you ask?'

'Sorry,  you were screaming in your sleep and I was concerned.'

'I am fine, thank you ...' I hid the fact that my entire body was covered in sweat and I was breathing quite heavily. 'And you?'

'I couldn't sleep. I never really sleep that well, to tell you the truth.'

I could fully relate. I looked around and still couldn't believe I was in a strange place in a strange land. It felt just like yesterday that I was in my bed back in the city. 'So, what are you doing with yourself? Drinking?'

'No, I don't drink, but I had something else in mind.'

'What did you have in mind?'

'Come, I will show you something.'

I threw off the blanket and turned around after seeing my shirtless self. The poor woman has clearly never been near many men before. But once I put on my shirt, she turned to face me. 'Show me what?'

'Come, I will show you.' She walked over to the left side of the wall to reveal a hidden door and a closet. As she disappeared into the mysterious room I got up and followed her into the small, three-by-three-metre room, which revealed a table with a worn-out Holy Bible sitting on it and a single candle lighting the room. Above the table was a crucifix. turned around to face me.

'You're Christians? How is that possible?'

'Our father introduced us to Christianity. He brought the crucifix from his travels worldwide.'

'I used to believe in God, but not anymore.'

'Why, what have you done?'

'Everything! ... I'm sorry. I know you will probably want to convince me that I am worth saving, but sadly, I am not.'

approached me and softly stroked my face. 'Poor man ...' She looked directly into my eyes and I stared into her beautiful brown eyes.

'Thank you and your family for your hospitality.'

'Our pleasure, we don't get much company.'

I started to smile. There was an awkward silence until our moment was interrupted by declaring, 'I should go and check if my family is okay.'

I let out an awkward cough. 'Yes, I think you should do that.'

Excuse me!' She brushed past me and left me in the dimly lit room to stare at the crucifix and the Bible. I let out a sigh before accidentally kicking the table, forcing the candle to fall on the Bible, setting it alight. 'No, no, no!'

I rushed to put out the flames, banging the Bible on the table. It opened.

*You were taught, with regards to your former way of life, to put off your old self, which is being corrupted by its deceitful desires; to be made new in the attitude of your minds: and to put on the new self, created to be like God in true righteousness and holiness. (Eph 4:22-24)*

I didn't know what that meant so I closed the book and left the room without thinking too much about it. I laid back on the rock-hard floor, thinking about what would come.

But before I could rest, I heard loud knocking on the door. Mark woke up. 'Jacob, what the hell's going on?'

The women rushed down the stairs. 'Boys, do not open that door! It's the patrols!'

But the knocks grew even louder, and I could not ignore them, so I approached the door and opened it. There was nothing. I peered out into the empty street.

*Bang! Bang! Bang!* Across the street, flashes were coming from the window of a house as an armoured Humvee pulled up, and more green men got out from the back and began entering the house.

I was in disbelief. 'What the hell is happening?'

'It's a raid. The Taliban must be on to us,' said Yasmin.

'Quick, we must help those people.' I was close to storming over there, but  pulled me aside. 'No!'

'There is nothing we can do for those people.'

She was right.

'We are no longer safe,' said Sara, opening the back door.

We all rushed outside into the cold streets.

'Alright,' said Marc, 'where do we head?'

But just as Yasmin was about to speak … 'More patrols!' Sara yelled frantically, and we all quickly dispersed to hide in an alleyway. Luckily, we were out of sight of the patrols. In front of us, we saw the bright white lights from an M1151 Enhanced Armament Carrier that rushed past us. It was equipped with a M2 laser turret on the top and the words *Shahada* inscribed on the Humvee door in black letters.

Ashilya tapped me and Marc on the shoulder. 'We need to be careful. Patrols are frequent at this time of night; use the shadows to blend in like rats.'

Marc and I nodded, and the group proceeded to move out. But as we were sneaking around, we noticed something in the distance: two Taliban troops heading towards twelve Afghan women in two rows like shepherds leading cattle, and in the back was another officer holding a baton. The front girls were holding signs written in Arabic, and judging by the look on Sara's, Yasmin's and 's faces, they were not impressed with what the signs said. Suddenly, one of the girls at the end of the line collapsed on the ground. A soldier at the end whacked the girl in the back of the end as blood poured out of her head, and quickly, the girl got back to her feet and began marching. The sight was sickening. It made my stomach turn. Mark turned to , who had seen many of these demonstrations before. 'I don't get it. What did they do?'

'They broke the laws.'

Many Afghan girls had to withstand beatings, rapes, domestic violence and all sorts of abuses under these this regime. Women were treated as second-class citizens, more objects than humans.

Alishya tried to get us moving. 'Come on, if you want your truck back, we need to get moving before sunrise!'

I must admit I was missing American Division City. Yes, we didn't have the best legal system. Still, it was certainly much more humane than here. We moved along, slipping in and out of corners and buildings until we finally reached our target. The Afghan army's military base was nothing more than an old metal hanger guarded by two Afghan soldiers holding A100 rifles.

I looked at the women. 'Okay, so how do you propose we get in there?'

'Allow me.' Alishya brushed past me and began sneaking around the building. Then, she managed to get behind one of the Afghan soldiers and struck like a cobra, grabbing him in a chokehold. However, the soldier discharged three blue bolts before she snapped the soldier's neck. The second soldier held up his rifle, ready to shoot, but Sara and Yasmin tackled him, knocking him to the ground. They began pounding him, possibly making up for the beating they had endured. The guards were down, and Yasmin and  slung the A100 rifles around their shoulders.

Suddenly, Yasmin looked over at the street corner as more Humvees and armament carriers rushed down the street. 'Quick! Let's open the hanger and get out of here!'

Suddenly, the hanger opened, but we were caught entirely off-guard as we thought the place was not guarded. It turned out there were two troops stationed inside.

Yasmin quickly slung her rifle from her shoulder. *Pew! Pew! Pew!* She fired three blue bolts, taking out the two guards. Their bodies hit the floor. I now realised that these women were not to be messed with.

But the blast alerted the base and red sirens went off. More troops came rushing in. Twelve soldiers quickly entered the hanger and a firefight ensued with the women holding their own. Luckily, we managed to find cover behind laser-proof Humvees. Blue bolts flew in every direction, flying back and forth through the air. I wanted to help them, but Mark and I had no weaponry to combat them. We couldn't reach the weapons, as the bolts would cut us down if we tried.

'Jacob, quickly poke your head up and see if you can see the truck.'

I quickly stuck my head up and looked around, and for a moment, I could see the truck behind the soldiers. We definitely couldn't get past without taking them out.

'Jacob, did you see the truck?'

'I did, but we must get through the troopers on the other side.'

All five of us hurled ourselves down on the ground as the bolts went flying overhead,

It seemed impossible. 'I hate to say it, but I think this is it. I think this is where we surrender.'

But Sara wasn't having that. 'No, it's not!' She snatched the rifle from Yasmine, who cried out, 'Mum, what are you doing?'

'Quickly, get to the truck. I will lay down cover fire.'

'Sara, you don't have to do that!' I shouted.

'I do ... take care of my daughters for me, Jacob.'

I don't know what surprised me most – the fact that she was about to lay down her life for us or that she knew my name.

'Go!' Sara pulled her entire body from undercover and began opening fire towards the soldiers, grabbing their full attention. Meanwhile, Yasmin, , Marc and I quickly ran as fast as we could to the other side, ducking and weaving through military equipment. One thing we had going for us was that the hangar was poorly lit, and there was too much military equipment scattered around it for them to see us. Sara's distraction worked; the troops thought we are still behind covers and would not have suspected that we could break through their wall of plasma. Yet, we made it!  Right before us was the silver metal truck. Once we reached the truck, we quickly turned around to see the line of troopers still shooting at Sara, completely unaware that we were behind them.

called out, 'Okay Mother, quick, get over here!' But it was a stupid move as the troops quickly turned around and they all pointed their guns at us. All we could do was put our hands up in the air. But Sara threw a metal ball.

'Grenade! Get down!' The line of troops quickly dispersed as a tiny fireball ripped the barrier.

I yelled, 'Sara! Get over here!'

Sara nodded and ran for it, thinking she was in the clear. But unfortunately, one of the bolts hit her in the chest, and because she wasn't wearing body armour, it killed her instantly.

'Mother!' Yasmin burst into tears and her face turned a dark red from the pain. 'You bastard!' She wanted to rush out, but was stopped by her sister. 'Yasmin, don't.'

'Let go, !'

'No!'

'You can't help her now. She is gone.' hugged her. 'We have to go!'

I looked at Marc. 'Come on, Marc, get this bloody truck open!'

'Hold your horses, Jacob, I'm working on it.' Then, success! Mark managed to open the backdoor, and we all rushed into the cargo hold while the troops continued to fire just as the truck door closed. Luckily, the truck is heavily armoured and the bolts were not strong enough to pierce the armour.

Ashilya hugged her grieving sister as Yasmin collapsed on the floor in tears. 'Come here Yasmin, come here!'

It broke my heart. 'Can I say something?'

Ashilya and Jasmin looked up, confused that a stranger, who barely knew them for a day, was going to say something about their mother, yet they didn't interject. 'Look, I know it's hard to lose someone who meant the world to you, but we must keep moving forward. We can't save your mother's legacy if we give up now!'

The two sisters looked at me in shock that a male was showing them such compassion; even Mark was surprised.

Ashilya turned to her sister and whispered something to her in Arabic, which caused Yasmin to cry even louder. faced me and whispered softly, 'Thank you.'

But Marc was running out of patience. 'If you three are finished, we still need to get this truck out of here!'

I rushed to the passenger-side seat. 'Hang on, crew, this is going to be a bumpy ride!'

In an instant, Marc turned on the truck's ignition and rammed straight through the hanger door and raced down the road. At the same time, blue laser blasts hit the side of the truck. I love American engineering. 'So, how do we get out of here?'

Ashilya answered, 'We must go through the main gate.'

'But how will we open it? Guess we will have to go through the Afghan army!' Marc banged his steering wheel. 'I hate this place.'

I glared at him. 'Who cares about your truck, Marc? Let's just get out of here.'

'My cargo better be intact at the end. I am not going through this hell just to not get paid, which, by the way, Jacob, I am charging you for the extra passengers.'

I had to admit I was a little angry at Marc for his insensitivity, but I didn't really blame him. How could I? All the adventures he has been through have obviously made his heart as cold as ice; I guess Marc and I have something in common.

'There it is! The door out of here!' Ashilya pointed to the massive metal vault door that was the only way in or out of this glass dome.

But as we pulled up to the front door, a Humvee rushed from the corner street and blocked our way; its turning pointed directly at us.

I looked at Marc. 'Blast, that turret would cut through us instantly. What do we do?'

There was silence. Suddenly, Yasmin took off her necklace, which consisted of a bullet hanging from a chain, and gave it to Ashilya. 'Keep the fight alive, sis!'

Yasmin stood up and clicked the button to open the cargo door.

'Yasmin, where are you going?!'

Yasmin rushed out the truck's door.'

'YASMIN!'

Meanwhile, there was a Mexican standoff between the truck and the Humvee; one wrong move, and it was over. So, we had to move, and now. I decided to duck in case the turret opened fire; it was locked onto us — if we drove, the turret would open fire. Then Marc floored it! He placed his foot on the accelerator, which caused the front wheel to spin rapidly. The turret started warming up instantly, preparing to unleash a wave of bolts. Then, like before, Marc put the truck in reverse, and it shot back like a bullet, as the turret opened fire. Blue bolts instantly pierced the window, killing Marc and leaving his corpse to lie on the steering wheel. The truck came to a complete stop, and five soldiers quickly flanked us, opening up the cargo door and pointing their A100 rifle at us. 'شرطة (كرويين)، ارمي سلاحك' (Drop your weapons).

I didn't understand what they were saying, but Ashilya did, and she held up her hands, so I decided to follow her. So, we stood there, and the commander gestured for us to come out. Not wanting to cause trouble, we slowly advanced. But there was something peculiar, one of the many cargo boxes was open, and as I walked past, I noticed that the box was completely empty. Ashilya and I began slowly exiting the building when a missile suddenly flew past our truck and *bang!* The missile instantly destroyed the Humvee, leaving nothing but a fireball in its tracks. What was that!

We both looked at the source of the missile and saw Yasmin standing in front of the window, holding an ATGM launcher. It turns out the sisters managed to salvage one thing. Yasmin dropped the launcher on the floor as she only had one missile. Suddenly, the house came under fire as more and more troops arrived at the scene, and more were coming in the distance. I could see more Humvees arriving. The last we saw of Yasmin was her running way from the window.

Mark's body to the side, I jumped into the driver's seat and accelerated towards the gates.

'Wait!' rushed up to the cock-pit, grabbing my arm in a plea for mercy. 'We have to go back for my sister.'

'No! No time. The troops are gaining on us!'

She tried reaching for the wheel, but I had to push her back as their house slowly began fading from sight. 'YASMIN!' Tears rolled down her face.

I felt so sorry for her. In an hour, she had lost all of her family. I didn't want to do that, but we only had a small window of opportunity to escape. If we didn't move now, we would be trapped in this dome and possibly killed.

With one hard push, the truck flew as fast as it could, and then, *bang!* Back into the Wasteland we flew. A giant metal shutterer shot up in a millisecond, sealing up the inside as our windscreen was destroyed. But the only issue was that I couldn't see the road ahead. The whole experience got my heart pumping. Then, I heard a sound from above. 'Ah hell!' I thought to myself as the cockpit was blasted with those annoying sprays. The windshield was beyond repair, and the lasers had pierced the windscreen, meaning we would have to drive with this metal shield. Luckily, with a navigation system built into the truck, we could drive it without even having to drive it at all. It's crazy how far technology has come. I took more deep breaths, thankful to be alive … again.

But then it dawned on me that I still had an agitated female passenger curled up in a ball, crying. I should say something. When I got out of the seat, I slowly approached her with an outstretched hand, but I didn't say anything at first. Then I blurted out a small, 'Hey …', and at that moment, the crying stopped and there was nothing but silence.

'Hey, how are—'

 got to her feet, rushed over to me and began banging my chest. 'You bastard! You bastard. How could you?' Tears rushed down her face as her slapping weakened. At that moment, I hugged her, and her face leaned on my shoulder.

'It's okay. It's okay.'

'It's just so hard, I mean, how could I live with myself?'

'I know … Look, I am sorry I had to do it. You couldn't help your family by dying.'

She began to cry harder on my shoulder. After a few minutes of crying,  sat down in her seat, completely tired from crying. I wished I could give her more words of encouragement, but neither of us knew how to talk to each other as we were still complete strangers.  just looked down at her hands. While I, on the other hand, slowly began dragging Marc's body out into the cargo hold.

'Sorry about your friend.'

'Thanks, I didn't really know the guy, but he seemed like a good man.'

'How long did you know him for?'

'A day or two, poor guy. I felt for him.'

'How are you holding up?'

'Honestly, Jacob, I am really struggling. I mean, why me? Why am I the only one to survive?'

'I understand how that feels.'

'No, you don't.'

'Yes, I do!'

'Look, I have lost everything too. I know what it's like. I lost everything ... I lost my family, my friends, the woman I loved, and now, I feel like an aimless wanderer, like you, not knowing if I'll see tomorrow or if I'll see my family again.'

 looked down at her hands again. 'I am sorry.'

'We are survivors; it comes with the territory.'

She just gave an awkward smirk. 'I am feeling tired. I might rest out back.'

'Are you sure you're alright?'

She said nothing, just got up and returned to the cargo hold.

I was feeling fine at first as I got back to my seat, but an unfamiliar feeling hit me all at once; I felt so weak and afraid. I tried to calm myself by looking around, then I accidentally hit the dashboard of the truck, and a small picture landed in my hand. I picked it up and turned it around. It was a younger version of Marc hugging his beautiful wife while standing out the front of their house. The craziest thing was that young Marc looked exactly like me; it was like looking into a mirror, but as I looked at the picture, it occurred to me that Marc's dead body was lying there in the cargo hold, all alone without any family around him. I could feel the fear creeping down my spine, and at that point, I lost it; I burst into tears and banged the steering wheel, screaming at the top of my lungs as I yelled out all sorts of profanities.

The pain of losing Mark and the pain of losing it all just hit me all at once. It was getting too much to deal with, and I was afraid. I just wanted to be home; I didn't want any of this. And without any strength left, I collapsed onto the steering wheel. I regained my composure and sat there in silence, not wanting to do or say anything.

'Are you okay?'

I turned around to find Ashilya near the cargo hold door, just staring at me, concerned, worried about me.

'Yer kid, I am fine, what about you?'

'Still tired—'

'Yer ... life does that to you, doesn't it? I just need some sleep, that's all.'

'I think we should bury your friend.'

'Yes, you're right.' I went out back and picked up Marc's body, placing it into the empty cargo box to seal it up as his own personal coffin. Out of respect for Marc's and 's families, we had a moment of silence as  began to pray in her native tongue. I had to admit I was starting to like  – she was a very kind woman, despite what she had been through. After the wake, there was no point sleeping, so we went to the cockpit and sat there looking at the metal shutters.

She broke the silence. 'So, where are we heading?'

'I have no idea, but we have to keep going.'

'Go where? We can't even see the road ahead.'

'We don't need to with navigation and autopilot. We will have to rely on the truck to get us to where we need to go, or at least I hope so.'

Ashilya grimaced. 'Are you sure this truck will get us where we need to go?'

'Guess we will have to rely on faith, not sight, to get us to where we need to go.'

I looked at Ashilya and smiled. 'All part of the journey, I guess.' My fear quickly turned to excitement. Oh well, I was undoubtedly going to die, but at least I had some company. While that fear still lingered subconsciously, I knew it was our only shot at getting back home.

'Okay, so here is the plan. I have some cargo to deliver; it is the least I can do for Marc, so we need to head to Asian

Division City. That is my only shot for me to get back home, and I can take you back with me.'

'Are you sure we will make it?'

'Who can be sure of anything? I am an American citizen. If you come with me, and we make it, I can help support you and give you a fresh start in America.'

She took a while, but it was her best chance. 'Okay, I am in! Let's get this done!'

I strapped in and started the truck, then switched on the navigation and autopilot, and the truck burst into gear and off we went. But before I could focus, I looked at the photo of Marc. I noticed an inscription on the back and it read: *For we walk by faith, not sight* (2 Cor 5:7) (KJV). I threw the picture down near my seat and focused on the navigation screen.

# CHAPTER 5

'**SORRY FOR KIDNAPPING** you and your friend,' blurted out.

I looked at her and smiled. 'That's okay, I now know why you did it. To be honest, I can't really blame you. You should be very proud ... your sister saved us.'

So, with nothing to do, I opened the driver's side storage compartment and found an entire bottle of Jack Daniels. 'Want some?'

She opened the bottle and skulled half of it. I was shocked. She handed the rest of the bottle to me, but I drank a little slower, yet enough to feel it hitting my head.

'So, how did an American like yourself end up out here?'

For the next thirty minutes, I explained my story ... how I started out as a factory worker before meeting a family who wanted to take down a giant corporation, WeapCo, a Multi-Billion dollar company that killed my friend family and nearly destroyed my community, which sent me on a political and military campaign to take them down. I succeeded but was blasted into the Wastelands ready to die. Thankfully, I was picked up by Marc. Now, I am stuck driving his truck to Asian Division City with a woman I only met for twenty-four hours ago.

'Boy, quite the adventure you went on!'

'Since we are asking questions, can I ask you one?'

'Shoot.'

'You grew up with no education, and your main language is Arabic – how do you and your family know how to speak English fluently? Hell, how do you know what America is?'

smiled. 'My father was an American English and Religion teacher. We were lucky – while we didn't receive a formal education, our father home-schooled us the best he could. We couldn't do maths to save our lives. Still, we could speak English as fluently as any American, except my mum, who could only speak Arabic. He hoped that we would leave our country to join him in America.'

'Interesting ... what happened to your father?'

'The Afghan Secret Police found out that he was an American national, and they beheaded him in the middle of the town square. Since then, it has been my mother and younger sister, and now I guess it's only me.' There was an awkward silence. 'Anyway, I guess we better get moving!'

I put my hand on hers in a sympathetic gesture, then quickly focused on accelerating. Ashilya leant on the passenger side door, trying to get some rest. The poor girl must be emotionally exhausted. But I had to stay alert even though I was still healing from my overdose. Nonetheless, I must persevere. I began slowly closing my eyes, and fell into unconsciousness. I kept hearing my name being called out: *Jacob! Jacob! Jacob!* Then I felt something push my shoulder gently. My eyes shot open, and it was my wife. I had these recurring flashbacks time and time again with my wife and child in a car, it wired though because I can't recall having a child but it felt like I did. I don't know what caused them, and I have the same dream, but one day, I will have to get to the bottom of it. *Jacob, are you still listening to me?* I rubbed my eyes, 'Sorry, I must have zoned out.' She did not look happy. *Damn it, Jacob, you never listen to me; it's like you're off on a different planet I mean, why are you never listening to me?* Confused, I flicked the car mirror to reveal the same boy from my previous hallucination staring at me with his seatbelt over his body. Then my wife just snapped her fingers in my face: *Jacob! Jacob! Damn it, why is it so hard for you to concentrate?* 'Sorry, what were we saying?' *Nothing! We were only just discussing the divorce papers?* 'Divorce papers, why?' *Because I can't do this anymore, Jacob; you never listen to me, and you always spend any free time we get together on your business ventures. It just–* She stopped by slamming her hands on her legs and resting on the car window. The poor girl was exhausted. *Just don't worry, just focus on the drive.* I stared out the windscreen at the beautiful dark and snowy mountains. I remember this when we were driving home from the policemen or, in this case, policewomen ball. I knew what was coming my way, but the only issue was that I didn't know where. There was an awkward silence as my son was just resting in the back seat using his tablet, and my wife and I just stared at the road. But we noticed something in the distance: headlights from a 2023 BMW, and it was speeding. My wife looked concerned: *What is that lunatic doing?* I shrugged. 'Must be in a hurry. Relax, I am sure we will have enough—look out!' The BMW came speeding down two double-yellow lines, forcing us to swerve off the road, hitting the speed catch, and pushing us down into the forest. As we were tumbling down the mountain, I heard a weird knocking noise coming from my head. The knock completely took my concentration, and then I heard the knock again; now I was confused, and finally, I heard the knock again and woke up completely.

I lifted my face from the wheel and saw a little girl standing at the other side of my window. *Hello, how are you today?*

I was utterly wired out; the girl looked as if she was a 10-year-old Caucasian with brown eyes and black hair with purple streaks. It was so strange; I must have been hallucinating. So, to check, I tapped on Ashilya's shoulder, who was asleep in the passenger seat. 'Ashilya, wake up.'

'What, what?'

I pointed to the girl at my window

The girl innocently waved at us again and said, 'Hello.'

'You can see her too, can't you?'

Ashilya looked shocked as she waved to the girl.

But then something caught my eye … pine trees were extinct years ago. How was this possible? The girl looked at me with a cheeky smile. 'What are you doing?' she asked.

'Where are we?' This looked like something out of a sci-fi movie.

lent over. 'Jacob, where did you drive us?'

'I have been driving for hours, I left it on auto-pilot but satellite navigation out here is tricky with the radiation out, so I don't know where we are .'

Ashilya was both angry at me and surprised that I could be so reckless by letting go of the control. But that rage soon dispersed after seeing the forest; her facial expression said it all. I didn't know what she was thinking, but I knew it must have been the same as mine. Was it real? But my attention quickly focused on the little girl in front of us, who kept smiling at us: 'What are you to doing in there? Are you two cuddling?'

'Little girl, do you mind giving us some room so that we can open the door?'

'Okay!' She stepped back a few feet. I knew it was a risk, but I had to try. I didn't know if the radiation would kill us, but I had to try. So, with my hand shaking from the fear of cooking, I clicked the button … Nothing happened … there was no cooking or burning lungs. I looked over at the Geiger counter, and no radiation level was detected in this place. There were trees as far as the eye could see; there was mist and green grass on the ground. We were in a jungle, not a concrete jungle, but a tropical rainforest. It was impossible, and it felt spectacular.

# CHAPTER 6

**I WAS OVERWHELMED** at the sight of it all. Never in my life have I seen real trees and greenery. Yes, we had artificial greenery in the city, but none looked and felt as pure as this. I felt on the air in my lungs, not that artificial stuff they feed us in the city, but actual oxygen, and it felt amazing. I wanted to feel real grass. Removing my shoes, I placed my feet on the ground, and the feeling sent a tingling sensation up my legs. I broke out into uncontrollable laughter as I looked around. But that was soon interrupted when I realised that I still had company, as the little girl was laughing at me.

'What are you doing?'

Just as I was about to answer, the warm sun beaming on my skin. Ashyila was enjoying it and smiling, too. I didn't know how this place was possible.

'Ha ha! You two are funny.'

I just smiled back at her. 'Little girl, do you mind telling us your name?'

'Of course, my name is Tilley, What's yours?'

'My name is Jacob ... Jacob Turner.'

extended an outstretched hand. 'And my name is . Hey, Tilley, where did you come from?'

She giggled. 'Come, I will take you to the station.'

'Station? What station?'

'Ha ha, come with me, and I will show you.'

I shrugged my shoulders at Ashilya, as she was just as confused as I was. Nonetheless, I didn't know where we were, so with no other option, I took one hand, and Ashilya the other, and the little girl began leading us deep into the forest. The light from the sun began to fade as the canopy of the trees prevented the sun's penetration, creating a dark void. Nonetheless, we weren't scared. I felt the mist on my face, and then I saw it ... no way was that a stream of clear water within the radiated Wastelands. What the hell?

Tilley stopped, and we all stared at it. Was that an electric charging station? Deep within a remote forest in a land that was supposed to be dead? Was my schizophrenia playing up again? I had to see this for myself. 'Tilley, can you take us inside?'

'Sure, follow me.'

Ashilya, Tilley and I walked up to the electric charging station, which, by the looks of it, also acted as a diner and repair shop as there was a giant red electric neon sign that said: *Marc & Co*. This was just getting weirder and weirder as the place was styled as one of those 1950s gas stations, which was cool, but why was it stationed here of all places? We peered through the window. The inside resembled a 1970s diner with red-and-white checked patterns, and in front of us stood an old counter with holographic projectors above it of various food items, and there were old seating booths. This scene reminded me of *Back to the Future Two*. It felt familiar, as if I had been here before. We opened the glass door only to be alerted by the *ding* of a rustic bell at the top of the door.

There was no one at first, then we heard from the back of the kitchen: 'I'm coming!'

The door into the kitchen swung open, and an old man of Eastern descent in his 50s, with grey hair, morbidly obese, and with a thick accent that tried to resemble an American accent. 'What would you like?'

Ashilya and I shot each other confused looks. I answered, 'Young Tilley directed us here.'

But before we could say anything, Tilley accidently lend over a bench and some dishes fell onto the floor with a crash

The man got furious. 'Agh! Tilley!'

A shivering Tilley approached the man. 'Sorry, Papa.'

The man said something in Arabic, and the poor girl ran into the kitchen crying. I didn't know this man, but I didn't like him.

'So sorry about that, she can be such a pest, that girl. Don't know why I adopted her.' The man tried to laugh it off, but we weren't impressed. Nonetheless, this was the only place, so we had no choice.

'Umm, what you got?' I enquired.

'Our all-American milkshakes are popular.'

'I guess we will take that!'

'Okay, both of you, it will be ready soon.'

Ashyila and I sat on the red rotating cafe stools. I asked the man, 'So, while we wait, can you tell us where we are?'

'Why you are in the best and only All-American Marc & Co Electric and Diner, perfect for travellers like yourself!'

The vendor turned around to focus on making the milkshakes. But I was still curious. 'So, how long have you been in the business?'

'Oh, about 1,000,000 years, give or take.'

That was strange. The guy looked to be in his 40s. 'How the hell did you survive for so long?'

He just smirked. 'The trees keep me young.' He slid the two strawberry milkshakes with ice cream and chocolate swirls towards us in vintage glasses.

But I didn't care about the milkshakes, I wanted to know what was happening. 'How are the trees keeping you young?'

The vendor stopped. 'It's a long story.'

'Go ahead, I have all the time in the world.'

'Well, it depends on how you propose paying for the milkshake.'

Ashyila and I sighed as we had no money to pay. The vendor knew and was angry. He slammed his hand on the counter. 'Goodbye and enjoy the milkshakes on the house!' He mumbled a profanity under his breath and began storming towards the kitchen.

As he was about to disappear, Ashyila spoke up, 'Wait! We have a truck that needs repair. We have lost our windscreen, and we are lost. Please, we have cargo we can spare as payment.'

The man was intrigued. 'What kind of cargo?'

'Weapons, American weapons!'

He smiled and laughed. 'Okay, I can have your truck repaired by tomorrow.'

'I don't see any mechanic around here,' I said.

'No need, I will repair it myself.'

'Really?'

'Yes, five thousand years teaches you a few things. Tilly will cook you both dinner while you wait. Tilley!'

Tilley came out of the kitchen smelling of grease and wearing an apron.

'Cook our guest all-American hamburgers and fries and make it snappy. Chop! Chop!'

Tilley sighed and walked back into the kitchen.

got up from the table. 'I will bring the truck around.'

I nodded, and off she went. So, while we waited, I asked the man, 'Can you tell us what's up with the trees and what the hell is going on?'

The vendor rubbed his chi and began, 'Before World War Three, the organisation of Islamic Cooperation was concerned as the oilfields ran dry. They were worried that without oil, their countries would be disregarded, and their economies would be left in ruins. The countries tried to work their economies into a mixed economy to survive. So, through collaboration, the nations began experimenting with nuclear radiation to terraform the land with experimental plants to convert the land into either farmland or forest to sell wood overseas. However, after the war, the Middle Eastern and Asian nations from Israel to India were wiped out in the nuclear war. From the ashes of the old world, the plants began to take over, transforming the land into baran and lifeless deserts into beautiful green forests. Amazingly, these plants were all radioactive and could absorb harmful radiation from within the air, making the land breathable and habitable. Incredible. We have lived in these domes our whole lives when there was habitable land around all along!' His face changed, and he shook his head' 'Those two nations, American Division City and Asian Division City, are too busy destroying each other, and too ignorant to see that the answers to the problem are right under their noses. But then again, who are we to judge?'

'I thought you love America?'

The vendor smirked. 'I loved what it used to be, the United States of America, the land of the home and free. I lived through the era of Reagan at a time when the world made sense. You know, when I was a kid, I used to admire America; I dreamed of opening my restaurant in America as my family grew up poor in Saudi Arabia, and when I finally got there … let's just say I was disappointed, I barely could afford rent let alone open my restaurant. But now, after centuries of waiting, I have finally built my restaurant.'

I didn't care, as this situation was so bizarre and stupid. I wanted to get our truck and get out of here. But then a sense of unease struck me, deep within my soul, as I sat in the diner. There was something strange about this place. Outside, acid rain began to fall; I was trying to figure out what was happening as the light became overwhelmingly bright. I was anxious, and then I heard that song! I remember this place, I remember it! I began experiencing déjà vu as I started having flashbacks to this exact same café. I remember I was dressed in a fancy business suit, and my wife, dressed in a beautiful black and red dress with her hair done up nicely, approached the counter.

"Excuse me, please?"

The same man from earlier shuffled out of the kitchen, wiping his hands. "Yeah, yeah, I'm coming. What's the problem?"

"Our son needs the bathroom. Can he use it?"

"Restrooms are for customers only. You'll need to buy something."

"Fine. What's the cheapest thing on the menu?"

"A strawberry milkshake, $5.99. Or a burger for $12.99. Milkshakes are popular."

"We'll take two milkshakes. Do you take card?"

"Cash only."

That's when my wife snapped. "Forget it—we'll go somewhere else if you're going to be rude."

Something in me felt caught in a loop, as if I'd argued this exact scene before. My own voice cut through without hesitation: "Just pay the man so our son can use the bathroom."

"Jacob, I don't have cash."

"Then I'll pay."

"You don't have to turn everything into a fight!"

"Are you kidding me? We've got a kid screaming in the car. Let's just buy the milkshake and get out."

"Don't use that tone with me!"

"I'm not—I just don't want to make this bigger than it is. It's simple."

"Damn it, Jacob, I'm sick of you always blaming me—"

A sharp *Honk! Honk!* cut her off. Through the rain-streaked window I saw the old car—the same one that would later crash. Its yellow headlights sliced through the storm. A boy sat behind the wheel, leaning on the horn, urging us to hurry.

My wife threw her hands up. "Now our son's losing patience!"

"Then I'll pay so we can leave."

"Fine. Do what you want. I'll wait in the car."

She pushed through the door into the storm. I stood frozen, staring at the diner's stained-glass window, as the honking grew louder. *Honk. Honk. Honk.*

And then—just like that—I snapped awake. It wasn't a car at all but the truck driver leaning on his horn.

"Jacob," my wife said, "he told us he'd fix the truck in the morning. We can camp here tonight."

I turned back toward the diner—but it was abandoned. Not a soul inside.

honked the horn, getting impatient. 'Well, are you coming? No point staying here.'

So, looking back one last time, I stepped out into the dark and rainy night, not even concerned about my burger and milkshake. Oh well, it didn't matter as I wasn't hungry anyway. 'Coming now, !'

The rain was heavy. It was remarkable that the acid rain wasn't damaging the trees; it wasn't even touching me, as the trees made a perfect shield. The only reason I knew it was raining was the sound. What are these trees? They looked like pine trees, but they were something else entirely.  and I sat in the cargo bay with the door left open as the dim light lit up the entire cargo bay. We looked out into the dark forest, enjoying the oxygen while we had it. The two of us decided to eat the MRE packs – it was the only chance we'd had to eat on this entire trip. Ashilya was eating Mediterranean lamb while I was eating green curry.

We both sat awkwardly, neither knowing how to converse, as we were still complete strangers. But I must admit, looked naturally beautiful, wearing a white tank top, camouflage pants, and army boots. On the other hand, I was still wearing my worn-out body armour that I had been wearing since the start of this adventure, except the paint had worn off, leaving a blackish colour. Another negative thing is that I hadn't shaved since landing, so I was rocking a brown commander beard. What you notice when you have some free time to kill is funny.

I didn't know what to say as I wasn't the best at socialising. But luckily, broke the silence, 'Hell of a trip?'

'I guess you can say that, but I wouldn't say it was a good trip either.'

She just giggled at that comment; she had such a beautiful smile.

'How are you holding up with everything, kid?'

'It's hard! I can't comprehend that everything I once knew and loved is gone!'

'Don't worry, kid, it gets easier.'

She shook her head. 'Spoken like a true American.'

'Hey, my life hasn't been what you think it's been. Just because I came from a rich country doesn't mean I had it any easier.'

'So, tell me more about what your life was like before this.'

'Well, I had a girl I loved, but she became paralysed. I had a mum who became a politician and lost it to a corrupt system, and let's see … oh yes, I had a best friend who shot me and ended up killed on my couch right in front of me.'

She just smirked. 'Must have been nice to have an education, a job, and opportunities; my family got none of that; we had to fight for everything in this world only to have it lost or taken from us. And now I am stuck in this metal cargo truck with some American who couldn't even find Afghanistan on a map.'

I was taken aback at that comment, but tried to make fun of it. 'At least he isn't that bad looking!'

She laughed. 'Boys!'

I was about to say something, but we heard a knock on the right-hand side of the truck. Both of us shot up from our seats in shock and grabbed our rifles. But we heard a young voice say, 'Excuse me!' I jumped down as hid in the cargo bay.

'Hello, are you there?'

I turned around to find Tilley standing outside holding a metal box. 'Tilley?'

'I brought you something,' she said.

'Hi Tilley, get in. Isn't it dangerous for a young girl like yourself to be out here?'

Tilley hopped into the cargo bay.

'Tilley, what are you doing here?' asked .

'I brought you something.'

I opened the box to find three hamburgers in sesame seed buns, tomato, ketchup, mustard, pickles and cheeses served with three boxes of fries and three strawberry milkshakes.

'You left without your food.'

'Thank you, Tilley,' said , 'but you have to join us!'

We threw away the MRE for the burgers and sat around eating and drinking.

'Tilley, why did you come to give us this food? You know what you did was incredibly risky.'

looked at me. 'Jacob, she is just a kid, so don't be hard on her.'

'It's okay. I do it all the time.'

I nodded. 'So, what's up with your father? Why is he so mean?'

Tilley looked down at her burger. 'He is struggling a little bit; the old age is getting to him. He does it out of love, I guess.'

enjoyed her burger. 'Tilley, this is delicious; you made this?'

'Oh yes, Father has me cooking in his restaurant, so I guess you can say I have been practising.'

I was shocked that someone so young was working a full-time job. But then again, I couldn't talk. I served in the military before the age of eighteen. We all got to do things we didn't want to do as kids.

'Well, young lady, this was delicious; hats off to you.'

'Thanks.'

I broke the niceties. 'It's getting dark, Tilley, you shouldn't be out alone; it's too dangerous, and your father must be wor-ried sick.'

frowned at me. 'Ignore grumpy pants there; you can stay here as long as you like.'

Tilley looked at  and turned her head to one side. 'I like you – you seem nice.'

I kept up my interrogation. 'So, Tilley, how long have you been at this restaurant?'

'I don't know. I guess I was born here.'

'No mother?'

'I don't know, I never met her. I was abandoned here, at least that's what my father says.'

'I am sorry, kid.'

wasn't impressed because she knew what kind of man Tilley's adoptive father was. She knew he was only exploiting her. She was disgusted; she hated people who used innocent girls like her as slave labour. Especially someone so young.

I knew we had to keep moving. 'So, Tilley, do you know exactly where we are?'

'No, I have never—' Tilley noticed the two rifles in the corner, which saddened her. You're here to kill us, ain't you?'

'No, Tilley, we are not. We would never want to hurt you or your family.'

'Then why are you here?'

'Well, Tilley, the truth is that we are lost and are trying to reach our destination but don't know how to get there.'

'Maybe the tree can help you?'

'There are trees all around us.'

Tilley giggled. 'No, silly, come, I will show you!' She jumped out of the truck and began running. 'Are you coming?'

' and I shrugged and hopped out of the truck to follow her. We ran as fast as we could, with Tilley running deeper into the forest, and the forest got darker and darker. But the only thing guiding us was Tilley's voice. 'Come on! You are going to miss it!'

We ran until darkness surrounded us and we saw it — a green light that pierced the veil of darkness.  and I slowly made our way towards the light, and once we stood there, we saw the tree that Tilley was guiding us to.

This tree was encircled by smaller trees in the centre of the forest. But this tree was different from the others as it was oak and it was glowing with a green, radiant light that radiated a warm glow. I felt a rush of peace coursing over my body. But when I looked down, I noticed my veins were glowing green, similar to when I took . What the hell was this tree? The glow surged through my body, strengthening every cell and waking my mind.

I stood there admiring its beauty until I heard the voices, possibly from the tree, calling to me. So, I slowly began to walk closer and closer as the voices grew louder and louder. Once I reached the tree, my mind was overcome with a blurry premonition as I replayed the crash repeatedly, the same old memory like a broken— Hang on! What was that? As the memory replayed, I noticed something – my consciousness woke up from the steering wheel covered in blood as glass lay everywhere. It was a weird feeling as I couldn't move and had no control over my actions; I just had to watch it like a twisted horror movie. I watched myself turn around to look at the backseat to find my son dead, covered in blood, and as I turned to the passenger side, I found my dead wife with her white eyes just staring at me. All I could remember was screaming in pain and crying at the sight. The memory felt so painful that I could feel it even now. *Agh!* The scream was so painful that I snapped out of it, and I broke into a breathing fit as my heart felt like it was breaking out of my chest. I opened my eyes to find my hand placed directly on the tree. I turned around to find  and Tilley staring behind me, and I could tell they were concerned. I was about to head towards them when I heard a sinister laugh from the tree, *He he he!* It was loud enough to cut through the forest. Where was that coming from? Suddenly, a green laser bolt blasted straight into Tilley, leaving a burning imprint on her back as she lay on the forest floor.

Ashley let out a dramatic, 'No!' as she rushed towards Tilley's dead body, hugging her, hoping for her to wake up. I heard that laugh again ... *you bastard!* I knew the voice instantly. Out of the forest, the vendor appeared from the trees with glowing green eyes and an evil smirk. It was the same man who was in the diner, except he now wore a black suit, undershirt and tie. His hair was combed over as he slowly began approaching me, completely ignoring and his dead daughter.

'Ah ha! You figured out the truth, Jacob Turner.'

Angered, Ashyila rushed at him with drenaline-fuelled strength and speed. However, the man quickly whacked  away with one hand, sending her flying straight into a pine tree with enough force to knock the tree over, leaving Ashyila unconscious.

'Stupid imaginary constructs! Thinking they can act for themselves, this is on you Jacob! That poor girl wouldn't have to die if you would just open your mind"

"But then again, I guess we are all a little blind to the truth.'

'You should know Jacob.'

'Who are you and how do you know my name?'

"What are you talking about?

'You know who I am, Jacob. I am what you want me to be! I am the darkness that lurks in your brain.'

'What does that mean?'

'You will figure it out!'

Angry, I lunged at him again, trying to strike him. But with an open palm, he pushed with just a fraction of his power, sending me flying through the dark forest, landing on the forest floor as I held my chest, struggling to breathe. He jumped up at least two feet, ready to strike me down; luckily, I was able to move out of his way and he left a massive crater on the ground where he landed. Man, he was powerful, for sure.

'What are you?'

'I am what gives me power!'

'Why do you want to kill me?'

'I don't want to kill you; I want you to leave!'

'Fine then, I will leave your forest in peace. Just let us leave!'

The vendor shook his head with a condescending smile. 'You still haven't got it'. Suddenly he turned, sensing something.

Ashyila fired multiple bolts at him. He stopped them in mid-air, and you could see the speed trail they left behind. The vendor flung them away and began telekinetically choking, lifting her like Darth Vader. If I were to defeat this guy, I would have to overpower him. So, I swung at him, punching him hard enough in the chest, not hard enough to take him out, but enough to send him flying a few metres, and sufficient to take his concentration off, which I was counting on. But he recovered quickly and levitated mid-air, his eyes glowing red.

shouted, 'You're evil! How could you kill that little girl?'

'You don't get it, do you, Jacob. If you want her back, bring her back!'

'Go over to her body and heal her. Use the tree to heal her.'

I was enraged by this guy, so using my eyes, I projected a green beam at him, the tree! The tree was giving me my powers again, it was like when I took Xenogen . I knew how this power worked from my fight with John. But he just held up his open hand, absorbing the energy and rendering the attack useless.

'Come on, Jacob! Get creative! Where is your imagination?'

I looked over at , who was nursing Tilley's dead body. If I was to beat this guy, then I would need to use my brain, so slowly I began to breathe heavily. If only I had a sword or something that I could use. But then I looked down at my right hand and there it was ... in the right palm of my hand was a Samurai sword, rusted yet functional.

The vendor let out his sinister laugh. 'Good Jacob, you're learning. If only you knew the power that you possess! Wake up!'

The vendor's hand generated a knight's sword and came charging at me with enough force that he forced me to lean back. I tried to strike back, but he was too strong. There was no way of taking him down. I wasn't concentrating on the fight, as all the time I was thinking about Tilley. I wanted to bring her back, but how? Out of nowhere, Tilley jumped on the vendor like a wild animal and began striking him, which gave me enough time.

I quickly rushed to the tree, but as I got closer and closer, my head began to hurt. I could feel dizziness coursing through my body. The roots started to grow bigger and glow greener. It felt as if my spirit and flesh were separate, and I could feel my mind beginning to transcend my earthly body.

The vendor laughed. 'So good to get to the tree … learn from it … use its power to defeat me! Free yourself!'

I stopped for a minute. 'I do have the power, but I will not use it on you!' I quickly turned to  and Tilley. 'Ladies, I have an idea … come to me!'

They both ran over to me, and we stood there in defiance of the vendor.

'Girls, are you ready?'

 yelled, 'Wait, Jacob, what are we doing?'

'I want the two of you, on the count of three, to picture burning that tree.'

They nodded.

'Ready! One! Two! Three!' Suddenly, three beams – a green one from my eyes, a red one from 's eyes and a blue one from Tilley's eyes – all struck the tree, forcing the vendor to scream out, 'No! You were meant to use its power to know the truth, instead your own arrogance has caused you to blindly destroy the thing that grants you power. "You stupid Constructs!' He slowly began marching towards us but looked down at his hands as they began to turn into dust. His body began to deteriorate.

Still, instead of screaming out in pain, the vendor just laughed. 'I will return when the time is right!' Then a pair of bat wings emerged from his back, and he flew up into the sky, travelling at the speed of light. The mighty oak tree was left to nothing but a crisp as the green glow from the tree roots died and the roots slowly shrivelled up and turned a black colour.

All three of us collapsed on the ground and we began to laugh. We were thankful that it was all over. But the effects of the tree had not left me as I felt a rush of pain surge through my head as memories kept flooding back of the same scenarios of the BMW forcing us to swerve off the road and into the exact same oak tree that was giving us power.

But, when I thought it was over, I heard the vendor's voice laughing. 'The more you suppress me, the more powerful I become! Sooner or later, Jacob, you will have to face the truth!'

But I ignored it. I turned to my friends as they lay exhausted. Then I saw that our truck was now fully repaired. The only good thing the vendor did for us was repair our vehicle. So, at least we had a working truck. I really wanted to get out of this place, I mean, it was beautiful, but it defied all logic and laws.

'Alright, , the truck is repaired, so let go!'

'Wait a minute, Jacob, what about Tilley?'

Tilley was standing there, looking sad. We turned our heads around so Tilley couldn't see us.

', this journey is no place for a child.'

'Jacob, she has no other family!'

I wanted to argue with her but couldn't. I was hesitant for a moment, but damn! 'Alright, kid, come along. We will take you to the city, but after that, you must find shelter somewhere else.'

Tilley shot up with joy. 'Yay!' She rushed over to me and gave me a big hug. I wanted to shrug her off, but I caved in and hugged her.

'Alright, get in the truck!'

Tilley opened the door and hopped in the back.

smiled at me. 'You're a good man, Jacob!'

I couldn't help but smile to myself. As I jumped into the truck, I looked over at the forest of trees as if something was not right. As the trees turned colouring from fresh green to dead brown, they were all dying. Also, I looked down at the ground and found the grass was turning brown. I had better not waste any more time getting out of here!

*Snap!* I peered out the windscreen, and I saw the mighty trees were falling. I slammed my foot on the accelerator and the truck flew into action.

'Quick, girls, you better strap in.'

Not arguing,  jumped into the passenger seat and fastened her seatbelt as Tilley held on tightly in the cargo bay. Rows upon rows of pine trees came falling down, roots and all. What was worse was their roots were being pulled out of the soil, making the ground uneven. If I didn't floor it now, this forest would be our tomb.

Man, the track was long and narrow, weaving in and out of trees; thank goodness this truck was an off-roader. I prayed hard that the engine didn't shut down or the tyres blew. But I could see the way out; it was a narrow entrance out into the desert, the only way out. As the scorching light from the radiated Wastelands shone through the ever-dark collapsing forest around us, it was like travelling through a tunnel. We needed to be quick as the exit was closing and the tree was falling fast; no time to waste with my speed gauge exceeding the recommended speed. Come on! Come on! We shot through the exit. Success! We made it!

Even though poor Tilley was in shock, as the speed shot her to the roof and back on the floor, she was a strong girl – she could handle it. There was silence for a second, realising that we nearly lost our lives, and then all three of us broke into laughter at the thought.

I breathed in deeply. 'Okay everyone, buckle up.'

 stayed in the passenger seat. Slowly, we kept moving into the Wastelands.

# CHAPTER 7

**I WATCHED AS** the trees slowly faded away, disappearing into the desert. She looked sad.

'Hey, are you okay?'

'I am just missing home, that's all.'

'Little advice, kid, we are battlers. We don't have the luxury of moving backwards. We just have to keep looking forward until the battle finally ends.'

reluctantly sloughed back in her seat, looking through the windscreen and letting out a disappointing sigh! 'Jacob, what's America like?'

'Big, dull, grey and boring. Why do you ask?'

'It's just when we were younger, we heard the story of America being the land of opportunities.'

'Well, sorry to break it to you, but that whole idea of being a utopia is a bunch of rubbish. The truth is it is a flawed and a hard place, just like everywhere else in the world.'

'Why do you hate it so much?'

'I don't hate it; it will always be my home, but I am just saying that it's not what it makes itself out to be. Trust me, kid, home isn't a country; home is what you make it to be.'

'Well, you're right. I have no home.'

There was an awkward silence, both a bit bummed out.

Suddenly, Tilley opened the back door. 'Hello.'

Blast, I forgot about Tilley for a couple of minutes.

Tilley innocently sat on 's lap. 'I like you! You're nice!'

'Thanks, cutie … you know, you remind me a lot of my little sister.'

'Oh, yes, what happened to her?'

There was silence in the room. I better break the silence. 'Actually, Tilley, can you be a good girl and go get me a Philips head screwdriver?'

Tilley shot up from her seat with a smile and rushed into the cargo hold.

was confused. 'We don't use Philips head screwdrivers anymore.'

I smiled. 'Ahh, I know, don't worry, my dad did that same trick on me. I spent almost two hours looking for something that didn't exist anymore while Dad just sat on the couch drinking beers. Good times!'

Tilley returned. 'Sorry Jacob, I couldn't find a Philips head.'

'That's okay, why don't you sit near ?'

'Nah, I am bored!' She walked up beside me and started clicking buttons. 'What does this button do?'

But now I was getting annoyed, so I slapped back her hand. 'Don't touch anything, go and sit back in the cargo pit. Now!'

She rushed back into the cargo hold crying and slamming the door.

wasn't impressed. 'Damn it, Jacob, why are you being so mean to her?'

'Time to learn what the real world is like. It's cold and mean, and she needs to get a clue, or else she is going to get us and herself killed … like your sister.' It was too late to take it back.

She stood up out of her seat and let out an expected, 'Screw you!' and stormed into the cargo hold. I needed to hear this, so I sneakily opened the cargo bay door and eased back in on the conversation. Tilley was crying, curled up using her arm to wipe away her tears.  gave her warm, affectionate cuddles.

'Why is he so mean?!'

'Ignore him Tilley, this world is full of angry people. You just have to drown them out and be yourself. You need to be strong. Would you like to braid my hair?'

The two began to laugh as Tilley tried her best to braid 's hair but ended up making her hair look like a bird's nest,

'So, what was your family like, Ash?'

'Well, my mother was a kind and caring woman, my father was like grumpy pants in the front, and my sister, well, was a lot like you. She was an entitled little brat but smart and lovely.'

'Do you miss them?'

'Every day … what about you, Tilley? What was your family like?'

'I never knew my mother; the only family I had was my father. But we never got to spend much time with him as all he did was get me to work and cook for him. Is Jacob your boyfriend?'

 smiled. 'No, nothing like that. To tell you the truth, I really don't know who he is.'

'Do you find him cute?'

'Very cute, but sssshh … don't tell him I said that.'.

At that moment I walked into the cargo bay. 'Tell me what?'

But the two of them slouched back and looked down at the ground.

I sighed. 'Look, Tilley, , I just want to apologise. I took out my frustration, and that was not cool; can you forgive me?'

Tilley walked up, ready to hit me, but instead, she hugged me, and just gave me a big smile. All I could do was give Tilley an even bigger hug. 'Mind if I join you? All this driving is doing my head in.'

'Sure, come and join us!'

We joined in a circle, but Tilley got out of her seat and decided to go rummaging through the storage, possibly looking for something fun to do.

smiled. 'Come, I need to show you something.'

Not knowing what to expect, I got up and followed her to the other side of the truck. She had found a bottle of whiskey, my favourite.

'Ha, well I'll be … Where did you find this?'

'I noticed it earlier when I checked the cargo.'

'Makes sense. Marc must have all sorts of stuff stored in this truck.'

She winked at me. 'What do you say, cowboy? Can you handle your alcohol?'

I laughed. 'Oh child, I can drink you under the table any day.'

But before we could start drinking, Tilley returned holding an old wooden guitar.

I took it off Tilley and examined it. It was in good condition; even the strings were tuned.

'Come on, Jacob, your turn! What have you got for us?'

I walked into the driver's cockpit, leaving Tilley and  to wonder. The truck went from stainless steel to transparent instantly. I walked back in. 'Turns out this truck has a cloaking mode, so when you turn it on, it puts on a translucent clock, allowing us to see the outside.'

Tilley was impressed. 'Cool!'

looked at the beautiful night sky covered in stars and the cosmos. In front of us was the famous three-sided pyramid of Mount Everest. We were all blown away by the view.

We laughed and started playing with the guitar. We were lost in our little world, living for the moment.

'Okay, guys, give me the guitar.'  gestured for Tilley to hand the instrument to me.

'What? You play guitar?'

'I used to play a little for my sister. Here is a little song I used to sing to get her to bed. It's called *Da Zamong Zeba Watan* which in English means 'This is our beautiful home-land.' She took a deep breath in, and the guitar came to life.

*Da zemong zeba watan*
*Da zemong laila watan*
*Da Watan mo zaman dai*
*Da Afghanistan*

Tilley and I smiled.  played it and sang one more time while we hummed along:

*Da zemong zeba watan*
*Da zemong laila watan*
*Da Watan mo zaman dai*
*Da Afghanistan*

At that point, we all just burst out laughing. We were all having so much fun.

I sat up and reached for the guitar. 'I have one; pass the guitar.'

Tilley laughed. 'What do you want to sing?'

I smirked. 'Come on, I was a pretty good singer. I got top marks in music class. This is an old 21st-century song I used to listen to way back in my youth. I hope you enjoy *it.'*

'What's it called?' asked .

'*Wake me up, by Avicii.* But keep in mind, guys, I am a bit rusty.'

and Tilley sat back as I got ready. I strummed the guitar and took a deep breath in. I let my heart speak through my fingers:

*Feeling my way through the darkness*
*Guided by a beating heart*
*I can't tell where the journey will end*
*But I know where to start*
*They tell me I'm too young to understand*
*They say I'm caught up in a dream*
*Well, life will pass me by if I don't open up my eyes*
*Well, that's fine by me.*

 and Tilley looked at me, stunned – they obviously liked it, but then again, I couldn't tell.

*So wake me up when it's all over*
*When I'm wiser and I'm older*
*All this time, I was finding myself, and I*
*Didn't know I was lost.*

I stopped, and they both broke into applause.

'Jacob, that was beautiful!' said Tilley.

I smiled. 'Thanks, it was something I used to sing to myself when I had time.'

'Were you a musician in America?'

I shook my head. 'No, I was a manufacturer until my business burnt down. Now I am just a wanderer like you both.'

Tilley started to yawn.

'Time for bed, little lady.'

'Nah, I can hold on a little while longer; I just need to rest my eyes.' She laid on the ground, and in an instant, she was sound asleep.

 and I watched her 'Did you ever think about having kids, Jacob?'

'Me? No! I am not the marrying type.'

'Well, I reckon you should. You would make a great dad.'

I couldn't help but smile a little.

'Well, I better hit the sack. Good night, Jacob.'

'Hey , wait!'

She turned around in shock,

'We will find your family one day, I promise. I truly believe your sister survived, and we will find her one day!'

She kissed me on the cheek and curled up in a ball near the passenger window. 'Night!'

I joined her, laying my head beside her as I looked up at the night sky. Hoping that out there, Anna, my angel of a mother and Ella were still waiting for me.

The beautiful night sky was soon replaced with a virtually cloudy colourless sky, and the acid storm soon closed in with green-coloured raindrops bucketing down around us and the loud crack of thunder raging overhead.

I soon drifted off to sleep.

# CHAPTER 8

**SUDDENLY I HEARD** her voice: 'Jacob! Jacob! Wake up! I screamed so loud that it shot me up from my seat, and I looked around the truck. was still asleep on the passenger seat. The rain was bucketing down. It seemed like all that trauma and concussion over the years was finally catching up with me.

I knew I wasn't getting any more sleep tonight, so I switched on the truck, set it to manual, and drove off. Although the truck has auto-pilot, but I didn't trust it, as last time it sent us into a mysterious forest, and I am the kind of man who likes to be in control.

To get to Asian Division City, we had to go through Wuxi County in Southwest China, but it meant we had to travel through one of the most dangerous roads in the world, known as the Hanging Man Road, which got its name because travellers would be left hanging on the cliff edge and eventually fall to their death. Its original name was Lanying Cliff Road. It's a road caved into the side of a mountain. Still, it hadn't been maintained in the year, and even on good days it was treacherous, and given it was raining, it made the road even more dangerous. Nonetheless, it was the only way. I pulled up to the start of the road to find an old metal sign with Hanging Man Road written in red blood covering the sign, and what made it even more sinister was the skull on top of the sign – over-dramatic but still terrifying.

I stopped looking at the road and began contemplating whether or not to continue ahead as I had to think of 's and Tilley's safety; I took a deep breath. I realised there was no turning back, so I stepped on the electric pedal and moved slowly and swiftly onto the road. I looked ahead at the narrow road and the view of the mountainside, which was mostly covered in mist. As experienced truck drivers had died on this mountain, I was a little scared. I kept saying to myself, 'Don't look down, don't look down', as below was a one-thousand-metre drop onto jagged rocks. Slow! Slow!  The mountain was doing something to my head because I swear I saw a pair of giant bat wings flying past; it must just be my hallucinations.

But, as I was driving, I began to hear laughter, like a little boy laughing and my wife yelling at me and telling me about the police ball. I needed to clear my head, so I adjusted my mirror, and I saw the same boy, my son, looking at me straight in the mirror: 'Dad, can we stop and get something to eat?'

The vision freaked me out, and I accidentally turned the truck a little to the right and it dangled over a cliff edge. 'Oh no!' I was freaking out hard. I couldn't reverse as there was a mountainside blocking me, and if I moved even just the slightest, the truck could go face-first down off the cliff.

slowly opened her eyes, still weary from her slumber, but that all changed when she shot her eyes open. 'Jacob, what did you do?' She was stunned and shocked.

I heard a sinister laugh within my head. 'Ah! Ha-ha!'

'Vendor, what are you up to?'

'Go ahead, hero, use it! Unlock your mind and save yourself from the cliff below!'

'Shut up! I refuse to listen to you … you are merely a voice!'

'No, Jacob, I am more!'

My intense headache came rolling back, and the flashback played repeatedly of that same flashback of the BMW forcing us to swerve and run into the same oak tree. However, the picture was getting more straightforward and transparent; repeatedly, they played, but I was starting to make out the BMW driver, and as the BMW came speeding down … it was John! John Spear was driving the car.

The face of the BMW driver flashed between John's regular face and John's zombified face. It doesn't make sense. What does the CEO of WeapCo, the man who killed Yendan, paralysed Ella and destroyed my family, have to do with all these hallucinations? But before I could think,  snapped me out of it: 'Jacob, Get to the back of the truck!'

We quickly ran into the cargo bay. Poor Tilley woke with a start. 'Hey, hmmmm, what's going on!'

'No time. Quick, everyone stands at the back of the truck.'

No one argued and we quickly reached the back of the truck. There was a little shake. Thankfully, we could counterbalance the truck and save it from tipping over. Yet one problem remained: How were we meant to move the truck?

Then, an idea popped into my head: 'Guys, I have an idea?' I slowly walked over to the nearest storage container, and YES! I grabbed the MK160 and loaded our ticket to survival with a rocket launcher.

 wasconfused. 'Jacob, are you crazy? You could blow a hole in the mountain. It will send us over the edge.'

But I knew what I was doing. I quickly turned to the truck's right side and said, 'Fire in the hall!'

I blasted the rocket launcher, which shot the rocket into the distance to hit a random target. The velocity of the rocket blast shifted the truck a little, but I had to act fast. So, I quickly rushed to the driver's side, hit the reverse, and—breathing heavily—succeeded. The truck was back on the road! I reversed a little bit, and we were so lucky. A second more, and we would have plummeted to our death. Yet there was another problem: we now had a giant hole in the storage area. I yelled at the girls to hurry back inside, and they rushed into the truck's cockpit. I clicked the Emergency Decontamination button as Tilley and  rushed in the door. Within a second, the door to the cargo area was magnetically sealed up. The annoying spray blasted the cockpit. The good news was that we were safe and could continue driving; the bad news was we could not access the cargo bay until we opened it manually from the inside, which meant no access to food or weapons. No matter; we were not that far from Asian Division City.

We all stopped for a minute and breathed heavily.  began softly hitting me. 'What is wrong with you? You could have gotten us killed!'

'I am sorry, I didn't know what came over me!'

'Why didn't you talk to us?'

Tilley called out, 'Guys, can you please not fight?'

She was right. We had a mission to do, so I hopped back into the driver's seat,  into the passenger seat, and Tilley sitting behind  ... and we kept driving.

Thankfully, the driving conditions eased as the storm stopped. The journey was long and arduous, but it was worth it, as after we came out of the mountains, it was mainly flatland, and then after hours of driving, we saw the big concrete wall with the considerable glass dome overhead. It was similar to American Division City. We finally made it! I hadn't been here for years!

# CHAPTER 9

**ASIAN DIVISION CITY** is a metropolitan city surrounded by a massive concrete wall, covered by a twenty-storey dome, similar to that of American Division City. The town has a population of 600 million. Asian Division is the second biggest city on earth. It is considered second only to America, and its primary export is technology. We arrived at the border wall only to be met by a giant rusted-steel gate. We were escorted into a cargo bay.

A large Asian man wearing a high-vis jacket and a white hardhat approached us holding a tablet. In clear English, he said to us, 'Name?'

'Marc!'

The Asian man did not say anything and just clicked us off. 'Okay, would you like the money to go to the bank account on file or a different one?'

At first, I was tempted to take the money for myself, but it was Marc's truck and his delivery, so it would be a nice gift for his family. I sighed and replied, 'Account on file.'

Congratulations, Marc, your delivery has been made; now rest in peace, my friend; even though I barely knew you, you worked hard and put yourself on the line to provide for your family, which I respect.

I took a deep breath; it was great being back in Asian Division City.  and Tilley were excited as they were keen  to explore the big city. They had grown up in a small, rural areas and never got to see the city.

We stood at the loading station door, ready to see the sights that awaited. The doors swung open, and we were overwhelmed with lights and buildings. Asian Division City was a lot different to American Division City; the city was much cleaner and more sophisticated in terms of technology. It had artificial trees everywhere, and the bullet trains were so precise that they were never even a minute late. Billboards and drones were projecting advertising everywhere and creating art for the people. Still, the streets were crammed with people in suits. Asian and American divisions were similar; their skyscrapers were gigantic, even reaching the dome. But unlike America, Asia didn't have lower, middle and upper levels; they only had one level; in fact, the city was so big that families were crammed into a  mega-complex, as the land was essential and not a single inch was wasted.

After stepping out into the streets, we found street cuisines of different kinds. Tilley and  looked around like kids in a candy shop, taking everything in and trying whatever food they could find. It was remarkable to see how quickly this place had grown and changed. The last I saw of this place, it was decimated by American armed forces, and now it was a high-tech, vibrant metropolitan city.

We were fast approaching Dàoxù Street, and my head was beginning to hurt again as flashbacks returned. But this time, it was not of the car crash; instead, it was from my time in the war. Dàoxù Street was where machine-gun fire cut down all my friends and made me to hide underneath a car. I paused at the street sign and froze.

'Jacob, are you okay?' queried Tilley.

I quickly snapped out of it.

'Fine, let's 'keep moving.'

Tilley and  kept looking at each other as we kept moving forward down the street that used to be covered in debris and dead bodies. It was as if it never happened. Now, this place almost feels like a utopia, yet I couldn't help feeling we were being watched. I turned my head slightly and saw what looked like a Chinese soldier watching us from the nearest skyscraper. But when I looked over again, he was gone; I didn't know if it was my paranoia or if my brain was playing tricks on me. Nonetheless, I brushed it off and kept walking. 'Come on, girls, let's pick up the pace!'

But my body and mind became crippled with fear and regret as the memories of my friends dying like animals in the street began to remerge; I never thought I would be able to survive this place, let alone come back to it.

 tapped me on the shoulder. 'Hey, are you okay, Jacob?'

I stared at the street, and I wanted to tell her how I felt, but I couldn't, so I just shrugged it off with a simple, 'I'm fine', and continued walking down the street.

As we walked down the road, we were captivated by a beautiful red hanging lantern. Thousands of other people who were also taking in the nightlife. But the atmosphere was soon ruined when two Asian Division Secret Police stood before us holding SR600 rifles. I knew it was the secret police because they wore all-black body armour with the Asian Division flag and the iconic police symbol of two red dragons with a red star in the middle on a black background on the sleeve. A swarm of people rushed past like a swarm of fish around two sharks.

'Girls, we need to get moving.' I grabbed their hands and tried pulling them through the current of people, but at this point, we may as well be swimming in the ocean. I turned to find another officer coming behind us, slowly approaching as he shoved the pedestrians out of the way.

'Jacob, what is happening?'

', we have two officers in front of us and another behind us; we must keep moving.' She quickly turned to me. 'Jacob, what do we do?'

'Just keep walking.'

'Jacob, I am scared,' said Tilley.

'Don't worry! , Tilley, just keep moving ahead.'

Finally! We rushed down the nearest dark alley after pushing and fighting through the people. Excellent! This city was so clean. Even its darkest alley didn't have graffiti or smelt of piss. But as I turned around, the two officers were staring at us and slowly making their way towards the alley.

'Girls, run!'

We raced down the alley, trying to lose the officers. But they broke into running, and the chase began!

'Quick, girls, we need to lose them!' Turning around a corner, we ran to the nearest wall and began scaling it, using our momentum to grab the nearest fire escape stairwell. Tilley came close to falling, but I reached for her. 'Keep up, kid!'

We stopped to catch our breath but the officers trapped us. 'Stop, don't move!' Their voice projectors translated from Mandarin to English. 'Get off the fire exit now!' The second officer spoke into his radio. 'We have eyes on the Americans … I repeat, we have eyes on the Americans!'

There must have been a way to get out of there, but I could see none, so we all shot up our hands in defeat. Once we were on ground level, *Whack!* Tilley was knocked in the back of the head with a rifle butt. *Whack!* Ashley the same. I quickly turned to find three soldiers behind me. I hit the ground hard.

# CHAPTER 10

'AGH!' MY HEAD was throbbing with pain as I felt the blood rushing down the back of my head; I woke up in complete darkness, stuck in a mind-numbing void. I panicked.

'Hello?' I tried to move out of my chair, but it was no good as my hands and feet were tied to the chair with metal handcuffs so tight that they dug deep into my skin, and it began to bleed. All I could do was call out, 'Hello? Hello? Is there anyone out there?' But still no response; I was trapped in an empty room with no one but my thoughts to keep me company. So, in a last-ditch effort, I screamed out one last time, 'Hello!'

But this time, I heard something other than silence; I began to hear sobbing. 'Tilley? Tilley? Is that you, Tilley?'

The sobbing got louder and louder, but I began to hear the voice of a little boy. 'Tilley?' After all the crying, the voices stopped.

'Why did you let us die, Jacob?'

It was him again, the little boy in the car, trying to talk to me. 'Who are you?'

'You know who I am, Dad … you know!' The sweet boy's voice turned into a deep demonic tone. 'Say it!'

'Fredrick!' I blurted out without realising or controlling my outburst.

The sinister voice turned into a crackling laugh so deep it released glutamate into my brain, paralysing me in fear.

'What do you want? Please just leave me alone!'

'Oh no, Jacob, for I am just getting started!'

'What do you want with me?'

'You to expose the truth. I want you to suffer for what you did to that family.'

'I don't know who they are, and if so, what haven't I suffered enough?'

'You've created your own suffering, Jacob, which has only made me more powerful, and I will continue to grow in power until you break free. Ha-ha-ha-ha-ha!'

Suddenly, the bag over my head was quickly removed, and I found myself in an interrogation room. In front of me stood an officer of the Asian Division Secret Police dressed in his dark olive-green uniform covered in red emblems; there was silence in the room and then *Whack!* I felt the officer's hand slap my face.

'Now I will ask this of you, and you better answer correctly. Are you him?'

'Who?'

The officer wasn't amused, which I could tell by the death stare he gave me. Then, without any hesitation, he raised his hand and slapped my face again. I heard that same demonic laugh. I looked to my left at the one-way glass to find my own reflection staring at me, laughing with his demonic laugh. 'You don't have to take that; use your power to incinerate him!' Then, *whack!* Another slap in the face by the officer.

'Now, I will ask you this one last time!' The officer clicked on the interrogation table, and a hologram projected my face and my name. 'Is this you?'

'You know it is; why ask?'

'I need to confirm with my superiors. Is this you?'

I didn't say anything, which caused the officer to sigh, but if I didn't speak up, he would kill me. 'Yes, I am him.'

The officer stopped and changed the holographic projector to show a younger version of me hiding underneath a car. 'So, this is you?'

'Yes!'

The officer nodded to the one-way glass, and two officers came into the room and threw another black bag over my head. 'Thank you, Mr Turner, we have such uses for you.'

'Hey, where are you taking me? Where is  and Tilley? Where are you taking me?' I can honestly say I have been in so many of these situations throughout my life that I just don't bother to fight them anymore because if they wanted me to die, they would have shot me in the interrogation room. So, they obviously need me for something, but what?

'Jacob! Jacob!' I recognised the voice of .

The officers pulled off my mask and I saw  and Tilley on the ground in front of them with handguns pointed directly at their heads, and in the middle of them stood the captain of the secret police.

'Now Mr Turner, I know who you are and I know how important you are to our government's prosperity and safety. So, I am going to give you one last chance. Where is the resistance?'

'I don't even know what you are talking about!'

'Wrong answer!'

The officer shot the gun at Tilley's forehead, forcing both of us to flinch back in shock. Yet it was a miracle, as the bullet hovered just inches from her head, slowly turning but not even touching her as the captain stood back in shock.

'Oh my—' I looked down at my hands. 'Did I?'

elbowed the soldier in his groin and grabbed his rifle. *Bang! Bang! Bang!* Luckily, they were only stun rifles, so she didn't kill them. 'Quick, let's get out of here!'

'Where are we going to go! This place is crawling with police officers.'

'We will find a way out of here, won't we Tilley? ... Tilley?'

Tilley was crying as that was the first time she had ever been shot at, and for someone that young, it must have been traumatic.

'Oh Tilley, come here!'  gave Tilley a big hug.

But no time to waste as a laser bolt blasted into the interrogation chamber through the one-way mirror. We quickly ran through the door as we were outgunned; we threw down the metal table while  and Tilley jumped through the window to bolt the interrogation room door shut with the table wedged between the door and lock. All we could hear was the troops banging and bashing at the doors.

looked at me in a panic. 'Jacob, how do we get out of here?'

I looked around, panicked myself, thinking we were trapped in here, but luckily, my brain pulled through as I grabbed one of the rifle from the knocked out soldier and blasted a hole through the ceiling; I guess in situations like this, the only way is up! 'Tilley! ! Get into the vent.'

I lifted little Tilley first, then , and then the two helped lift me up. We slowly began making our way through the vent. But we only had a small window before the troops picked up that we were in the vent, so with a 'hurry-up' gesture from me, we all crawled as fast as we could, hearing the troops scrambling underneath us to try and find where we were. I thought we were in the clear, but the bolt above us began flying out of the metal from the vent, our weight causing the vent to come crumbling down onto the wooden desk below, breaking the ceiling above us as the troops gathered around in shock. I couldn't help but feel stupid that I thought this could work. The troops then surrounded us as Tilley, and I just stood there with our hands up; there had to be at least fifty officers surrounding us, each of them holding laser handguns capable of shooting bolts strong enough to cut us into a million pieces.

'Ha-ha-ha-ha!' The laughter was sinister. But whatever it was, it had definitely caught the attention of everyone in the police station, including us.

Suddenly, a clown's face projected onto every screen in the police station. *Boom!* A fireball blew through the front door of the police station, then … 'Smoke! Smoke!'

Canisters of smoke filled the room, covering the station and us in smoke. The police split into different groups to find the smoke's source. Suddenly, two blue bolts flew past the room, cutting down two officers in front of us, and then another! Eventually, the officers tried to return fire, but it was no good. They were being cut down around us at such a fast pace there was no point in even trying.

For the past five minutes, Tilley, and I crouched in the vent until there was silence and smoke in the room. We saw two soldiers clothed in dark-green camouflage and wearing gas masks. They carried plasma rifles and were scoping the room.

'Clear!' someone called out. The two soldiers looked at each other, walked away from the vent, and continued to scour the rest of the station; a third soldier approached us in the same uniform, except that this soldier had a sergeant strap on it. He crouched down to eye level with us. There was an awkward silence, then … 'It's been a while, Sergeant Jacob!'

'Who are you?'

The soldier removed her gas mask to reveal a beautiful Caucasian woman with brown hair, brown eyes and gorgeous tan skin. 'Oh, just a ghost!'

'Mackenzie?'

'It's been a long time, kiddo.'

'Mackenzie, is that really you?' Mackenzie and I went through the Academy together and served on two tours in the Pacific together. The last time I saw her was when our unit was pinned down by Asian Division Forces after our botched assault on Asian Division City; I thought she died all those years ago. But here she was in the flesh, alive and well.

'Well, Jacob, what are you waiting for? Get yourself and your friends up. Wait for my count … three, two, one … Go! Go! Go!' Mackenzie and her team quickly opened fire at the remaining forces. At the same time, , Tilley and I promptly bolted through the smoke and plasma fire, keeping our heads down and rushing towards the station's front door.

After making it outside, Mackenzie and two other masked soldiers followed behind us, returning fire into the station before joining us outside. 'Quick, we have to hurry before more forces come?'

'Mackenzie?'

'Jacob, no time to discuss; we must move now!'

, Tilley and I caught up as Mackenzie and her friends quickly rushed down the alleyway. It was hard to keep up, but we had to do our best because behind us, the police were radioing in more forces, and soon, this entire street would be locked down with more tanks and forces. We also had to be careful, as cameras were around each corner, so Mackenzie and her friends had to run and shoot. But Mackenzie was always a good marksman – top of her class in marksmanship, or should I say markspersonship and was considered the best sniper in our unit. She was still accurate as she managed to hit every camera that we passed with only a split second to react.

We must have run for thirty minutes, zig-zagging around all sorts of skyscrapers, going down back alleys until we finally stopped on the rooftop of an apartment complex where we all caught our breath. We breathed in as much oxygen as possible as our lungs burned. Mackenzie looked at me, gave me a smile, then a big hug. 'It's great to see you again, kid.'

We were the same age, but she called me a kid because she was the more sensible one.

'Likewise, Mackenzie, I thought you had died.'

'Come on, Jacob, you know I am too stubborn to die!'

Both of us burst into laughter at that comment.

'Tilley, , allow me to introduce you to my close friend, Sergeant Mackenzie Dunn.'

Mackenzie, and Tilley shook hands. 'Lovely meeting you all.' But then Mackenzie looked over at my face. 'You grew a beard, Jacob. I like it.'

I couldn't help but give her a big childish smile.

I never thought I would see Mackenzie again; we were like a dynamic duo – she was the sniper, and I was the medic. We were part of Seal Team 10, a highly elite radiation diver team that was responsible for conducting naval operations across the Pacific and throughout Oceania. We had been through so much: the Kangashark attack off the coast of Australia, the siege of Thailand, and the uprising of the Japanese islands. But nothing could prepare us for what we experienced on that grim day where we lost each other.

***

*Asian Division City, 3018 …* I led two teams comprising nineteen soldiers, including Mackenzie. After managing to capture the Port of Tianjin in a fierce battle, the American Division Defence Force coordinated a major operation comprising the air forces, navy and marines in an air and sea assault to infiltrate the city. While the army and space force tried to take the town through Old Hong Kong, it was one of the most significant military operations in our history, yet it was one of our greatest failure; known as Operation Retribution.

The American air force and navy, through heavy bombardment, managed to penetrate the radiation-proof concrete wall surrounding the city. At this point, Asian Division City was on the run, as the American Division Defence Force managed to push the Asian forces back to mainland China and out of the Pacific.  The Asian Division Air Force and navy had been crushed, and the city was at its weakest, or so we thought. Our team made our way through the city and into the capital. But it was an absolute bloodbath; the operation had turned into all-out warfare, building to building. There was fighting, and our hope was to create a surprise attack, and the army would infiltrate from the back, make a two-front war and entrap the city; that was until the Asian Division Defence Force managed to crush the American forces in Hong Kong and were doubling back, with a manpower of over 1.2 million soldiers. Anyway, the men and I were slowly making our way through the buildings, ensuring stealth. At the same time, Mackenzie watched our position from a nearby skyscraper. It wasn't going to be easy as we were poorly armoured. Most of these divers had just gotten out of training. Our communication with Command was limited, and the assault coordination was a shocker.

'Mackenzie, what's your position?'

'I am located on a skyscraper five clicks away."

'Make sure you watch out from the building as the enemy could come out of anywhere!'

'This is not my first rodeo, Jacob! Trust me, I have your back!'

This plan was going to work because, from the intel at the time, the Asian army was going on the defensive and protecting the capital at all costs. We were all walking through the rubble and mist of the bombed-out streets, which I later nicknamed 'The Lane of Hell'. The nineteen men followed closely behind with their rifles close to their chests. There was nothing except the occasional kids scattering into the shadow. Suddenly, I heard over the radio: 'Jacob, heads up, we have two men coming up on your position!'

Laser fire in front of us lit up from the nearest skyscraper as red bolts lit the night sky. The men quickly rushed behind anything that would give them cover, returning blue bolts in their direction. We managed to hold our ground, and after a five-minute firefight, we took out the soldiers, and the coast was clear. But after we had cleared the area, more soldiers came out of every angle; this time, we were struggling. However, we managed to take back the area thanks to Mackenzie's sniping skills. Until we heard clicks from every angle, and then, *vroom!* Bolts were flying everywhere, and our team was cut down; I only managed to escape because I hid under a car. The only soldiers remaining were Mackenzie and me; my heart was pounding. I could barely breathe or hear anything as the earpiece in my ear was ringing. The forces had overrun the city once again! Underneath the car, all I could see was the smoke from the laser fire, the dead bodies of my brothers and sister lying everywhere on the ground, and the black boots of soldiers marching down the road. Hundreds and hundreds of boots passed me, and then wheels from trucks and tanks rolled down the road; it was such a scary situation to the point that my body was paralysed with fear. I was hoping none of the soldiers would find me because if they did, I was dead. Then, while I was crouching under the car, my body decided to sneeze, which caused two black boots; they just stood there as the other soldiers walked around them. The soldier said something in Mandarin. I couldn't understand what he was saying. The soldier on his left crouched down and examined the car with a torch. He slowly moved down to look underneath while my heart pounded, then ... *Hello!* He shone the torch in my face.

I was a goner, but he didn't know how to act. I could see the fear in his young face as he screamed and quickly reached for his pistol while the soldier next to him freaked out. Then *ping!* A red bolt flew through the sky and hit the young soldier in the head, while the soldier to his right quickly scrambled to grab his rifle. But no luck, as that soldier was also cut down. Then, over the comms, I heard, 'Jacob, run!' I quickly rolled out from underneath the car. I ran towards the nearest destroyed building as more soldiers rushed by yelling out in Mandarin and shooting at Mackenzie's position.

'Mackenzie, what's your status?'

'Cut down and nowhere to escape, Jacob. I am scared!'

'Don't worry, Mackenzie. I am coming to get you.'

'No, Jacob, there is no point.'

'Mackenzie, don't be silly!'

'I am not; live to fight another day, Jacob. It has been an honour serving with you, Jacob.' The radio cut out, and silence filled the comm. I screamed in the air as my face went bright red, and my eyes filled up with tears. I wanted to run back and help her, but too many soldiers had too much firepower. So I ran as fast as I could, running through the buildings, running like a rat in the shadows, not knowing where I was going to go and what I was to do, but there was no point looking back, I had to keep moving forward.

***

'Jacob! Jacob!' I awoke from that memory and found Mackenzie snapping her fingers at me. 'Jacob!'

I was standing on that rooftop with Mackenzie, , Tilley, and all of Mackenzie's soldier friends, staring at me awkwardly.

To make a long story short, I escaped by returning to the Shanghai port in a mass evacuation conducted by the entire defence force of American Division City just hours before the Asian Division military managed to take back the continent and, within a year, regained lost territories in the Pacific. We underestimated Asian Division City's building capabilities and manpower as they were able to produce military equipment, tanks and weapons at such a rapid pace, and thanks to their population boom, they managed to outproduce us in a matter of weeks. Thank goodness they had a market crash within a year; otherwise, they would be the number one superpower. Also, the coordination between our forces was so poor that they crushed us on two fronts. In fact, their military grew so powerful that they managed to stalemate our forces in Europe and the Middle East in a matter of a year, rebuilding their entire military to the point that they reclaimed their spot as the second most significant military in the world, behind American Division City. Our chance at ever taking down Asian Division City was lost.

***

I refocused and noticed the other two soldiers as the one on the right spoke up: 'Excuse me, Mackenzie, but shouldn't we get back to base?' The soldier took off his mask to reveal an African-American man in his late-40s with balding hair and a blind eye.'

'Yer ... Levi's right.' The second soldier pulled off his mask to reveal a Chinese man in his mid-20s with black glasses and black hair. 'We need to get back to our hide-out.'

Mackenzie nodded. 'You're right. We should get back.'

'Mackenzie, are you going to introduce us?'

'Oh right … Tilley,  and Jacob, allow me to introduce you to my friends, Levi and Zhushan.'

The two soldiers nodded at us.

I didn't really care though. 'So, how are we getting out of here?'

'Well, here they come!' said Mackenzie.

We heard the rotor blades of a military helicopter descending from the sky towards the rooftop. The aircraft was an old version of a Blackhawk helicopter hovering within walking distance, but on the helicopter door was a flag; it was an old Chinese Republic flag with its red background, blue square and white star. The wind from the rotors was so strong that it created a wind blast that blew away dust and any item not attached around it. Then, the helicopter doors opened, and two soldiers dressed in Chinese soldier uniforms stood there, offering us a hand up. 'Hurry up, gang; we have drones closing in on our position, so let's move!'

We all rushed on board the helicopter, which quickly took off, but we were definitely not out of danger. In the cockpit, the two pilots were panicking as buttons were flashing everywhere. 'Behind us, there's a reaper drone!'

I saw a large MQ-10A reaper drone right behind us, ready to take the shot. But just as the drone shot a rocket, the pilot clicked a button and five flares shot out of the helicopter, which intercepted the missile. Tilley gripped 's shirt and placed her head close to her chest; this was no sight for a young girl.

'Quick, get on the turrets!' The two soldiers hopped on the pintle-mounted M150 plasma miniguns, which were located on each side, and began operating the current as the Torrent rotated for a couple of seconds and then shot six thousand bolts per minute. The drone was manoeuvring quickly, but after trying to pull up – *success!* The line of bolts cut down the drone in minutes, causing it to crash below.

We all cheered as the pilot flicked a few switches. 'Preparing to land now!'

The helicopter descended to ground level, landing next to an old 2025 Chinese bunker that was built out of solid cement and covered in vines. The location was invisible because it was situated between five skyscrapers and buried deep underground, which gave it the perfect cover as the helicopter touched down on the makeshift landing pad.

Two guards at the post in green camouflage equipped with laser rifles walked up to the chopper and approached the pilot, who declared, 'We have secured the package and are ready to see the commander.'

Mackenzie turned around and faced us. 'Tilley, and Jacob, you are to follow me!'

We followed them to the rusted door of the bunker and it slowly began to open. This bunker was designed in WWIII as a way for Chinese soldiers to hide from bombardment from the U.S. Air Force during the Battle of Beijing. We all walked through the door as the elevator slowly brought us down.

'Ladies and gentleman, welcome to the Republic Movement,' announced Mackenzie.

It was impossible; the Republic Movement dated back to ancient times. It was a movement that started on the island of Taiwan, hoping to form an independent country away from China. Still, I heard the remnants of the movement were destroyed once they pushed the American Division Forces out of mainland Asia. Still, that wasn't the case.

'Mackenzie, how many people are part of this operation?' I asked.

'We have over five hundred thousand people distributed globally in all sorts of splinter groups operating in every city from Europe to Asia and even America.'

'Our goal is to establish a new order under a new democratic republic built on the ideology and foundation of a free, democratically elected government.'

I took it all in as the elevator continued climbing. At some of the levels, soldiers were training with weapons, and throughout the bunker was all sorts of military equipment, ranging from helicopters to trucks and even the occasional tank. Still, there was always a Taiwanese flag on every level.

'Quite the operation you have here.'

'Just wait till you meet our commander.' As Mackenzie spoke, the elevator stopped, and the gates shot open. The corridor before me was decorated with yellow flowers; you could tell this building was ancient. In front of the Command Centre's entrance were two black magnetically sealed doors with two heavily armed soldiers standing guard – a complete contrast to the old decaying concrete around us. They jumped at our presence and approached Mackenzie. She held up a pass. 'We're cleared.' Both guards nodded, and one clicked the button. The doors slid open, and the light filtered through the doors.

Inside were state-of-the-art monitors and soldiers typing at every computer. I never realised how organised they were, as they had complete access to the entire security grid of Asian Division City; it must have taken years to hack the network. *Wow!* This was a site to behold.

'Mackenzie!' The commander of the organisation came walking from the big monitor towards us. He was a young Chinese man dressed in military overalls with a black shirt.

Mackenzie saluted. 'Jacob, , Tilley, I would like you to meet the leader of this operation, Commander Lin Zhengzhong.'

The commander reached out his hand to greet me.

'Wait … ZhengZhong? As in—'

'That's right! My father is Qin Zhengzhong, the president of Asian Division City!'

We all were shocked.

'Mackenzie, give them a tour if you don't mind.'

Mackenzie held her hand in the form of a saluted again. The commander did the same and walked away.

'Come, Jacob, I will give you all a tour.'

We made our way out of the highly secure bunker.

'Honestly, Mackenzie, I never expected you to be part of an organisation such as this.'

'This is the job, Jacob. It's a good cause, and the people of Asian Division City need this, you're lucky, your Americans you get the luxury of choosing your government, your religion and your own direction, we as Chinese citizen don't get that luxury. They live in a constant state of fear as police march through the streets using intimidation and military force against anyone as the government tighten it grip to prevent the people from talking out about the government and their ways of thinking, going house to house, crushing any sign of opposition they can find.'

'So how did this operation survive?'

'We stuck to the shadows, moved like rats, and thanks to the commander's influence, we remained undetected. But it's not just Asian Division City; we managed to reach every city – American Division, Europe Division, Africa Division, the Oceania outposts and even the Afghan villages.'

stopped walking. 'Wait, you have troops in Afghanistan?'

'Yep, and like you, we are helping to liberate people from those barbarians. I presume that is where you and Tilley are from?' "I did some background research on you two and Jacob filled me in on the details.

and Tilley went silent. Finally, after walking around the bunker for a couple of minutes, we stopped in an empty cafeteria.

I looked at Mackenzie. 'Wait, where is everyone?'

'Asleep!'

'Okay, so what are we doing in here?'

Mackenzie walked over to the cabinet and pulled out a bottle of whisky. 'We are catching up.'

 crashed out after two drinks, taking Tilley to a local barracks to sleep.

Mackenzie and I held our glasses, half-empty with whisky. 'What have you been up to since I have been gone, Jacob?'

'Left the military, got a job as a factory worker, started a political campaign with my mother and got involved with a military coupe to take down a giant corporation.'

Mackenzie shook her head. 'Honestly, Jacob, you have a knack for getting into trouble.'

She was right; *hell, the both of us seem to find trouble everywhere we go.*

'So, how's your mum Jacob?'

'Good – she became a politician.'

Mackenzie's face dropped. 'You're kidding! Anna?'

'Yep, that was until she got fired. Now I don't know what has happened to her.' I explained how I got from the desert to Asian City.

'Sounds like quite the adventure?'

'What about you, Mackenzie? How did you end up here?'

'After the operation ended in failure, I was sent to a re-education camp close to the border wall where I was tortured, beaten and broken physically and mentally. I spent a year in that gruelling place until I was busted out and recruited as part of the movement.'

'Do you trust them, Mackenzie?'

'Jacob, they are good people.'

'That may be so, but that doesn't mean they don't have ulterior motives. Trust me, I have been there.'

'Jacob, you had the luxury of the war ending, but for us, the war never stopped; for us, the war is never over, not until we win.'

'How did you survive anyway, Jacob?'

Embarrassed, I just looked down at my glass. 'I ran away!'

'Nothing to be ashamed of, Jacob – like I said all those years ago, live to fight for another day. Look, Jacob, I know you. You are like a brother to me, and I have been around you long enough to know how cynical you are, so trust me, they are good people, and it's a good cause, so let's leave it at that.'

We both returned to drinking the whisky.

'I must say you have changed a lot, Jacob.'

'How so? What is it? The beard?'

'That too, but your demeanour has changed a lot. When I first met you, you had a massive stick up your ass; you were like a robot – regimented – and you lacked any empathy whatsoever.'

'And now?'

'Now you seem at peace, despite what you have been through and are going through. You seem as if you do everything out of compassion for others.'

That made me smile and warmed my heart.

'So, what's the story with the girls?'

'They need my help, so I will help by giving them a new life in America.'

'Jacob—'

There was a knock at the door, and we turned around. Commander Zhengzhong was standing there. 'Mind if I come in?'

Mackenzie shot up and saluted. 'Commander, I—'

'Relax, I'm off-duty.'

'What can we do for you, sir?'

The commander showed what he had behind his back – a bottle of bourbon. 'I was hoping you would have another drink with me.'

The three of us sat in the dark, laughing our heads off and discussing old war stories.

Eventually, Mackenzie began to yawn. 'Alright, everyone, I have to head to bed. I have a class to teach. Night!'

Now, it was just me and the commander.

'Mackenzie's told me so much about you, and I hope you don't mind, but I also ran a background check on you – you are quite the person.'

'Likewise ... the president's son?'

'I would say more of the Supreme Leader's son. He was elected once and has never lost power since.'

'Regardless, that is quite the accomplishment?'

'No, it's not. It's more a curse than a blessing being associated with an evil monster.'

'What was it like?'

'It was like being an actor; all the camera shots and world trips had me being paraded to the masses as a puppet.'

This was surprising that a man who was basically descended from royalty would have such a negative view of his own father.

'Jacob, come for a walk with me. I want to show you something.'

The two of us downed the dregs of the whisky and the commander led me towards an old deserted tunnel covered in vines and left with barely any lighting.

'Sir, why did you bring me here?'

'This place has to be the most beautiful place in this bunker – you know why?'

I couldn't answer that question so I shook my head.

'... because even when the surface above is covered in desert and concrete, life finds a way to adapt and thrive, showcasing how resilient life is.'

I had no idea what this guy was going on about, so I just went with it. 'Can I ask you a question, Commander? He nodded. 'Why do you do this?'

There was a pause, and we just looked at the dark, empty corridor.

'Jacob, let me tell you a story. When I was younger, and my father had just been elected president, we would stop off at this small family restaurant run by a lovely couple in their 40s. When my father started off, he promised to be their saviour and save local businesses like his. At first, I thought he would save this business until I learnt the truth. Every day, when I was ten, I would sneak out and eat at that popular restaurant and order the same thing – Mapo tofu. Until one day, I found out that the government wanted to build a mega-block on the land and needed to destroy the restaurant, so the government sent in a construction team and built a massive brick wall around the restaurant, ruining everything that couple had worked hard to achieve. My father promised to save the restaurant, and instead he tore it down.'

'Sorry to hear that.'

'Jacob, because of my father, I lived a sheltered life and was given everything, but the issue with living a sheltered life is you are oblivious to the real world. It wasn't until my years in uni that I realised the truth – I discovered them ... the camps! Hundreds of them ... After seeing the condition of the camps, I grew to resent my father and everything he stood for. During my days in uni, I joined movements of all sorts, eventually rising through the ranks, until the American forces reached our shores; that is when I formed the movement.'

'My point, Jacob, is that people deserve freedom, and it is not going to be easily given. We need fighters like you to lead us to victory. So, Jacob, are you in?'

I thought about it for a second then offered an outstretched hand. 'Right, I'm in. I have been involved in many battles; what's one more?'

We shook hands, and just like that, I was now a recruit. 'Alright, well, I better get some rest.'

'I envy you ... I wish I had that luxury.'

But just as I was about to turn around, I noticed something about his eye colour; they had turned red, which scared me ... the Vendor? But I stared at his eyes again, and they turned back to brown.

'Jacob, are you alright?'

I stood back in shock and stared. 'Fine, I will see you in the morning.' That was weird, but it was best to ignore it, so I went to the barracks and found a bed. I guess I was a soldier again, which sucks because I wanted to get the girls home to American Division City. But at moment we were trapped here and miles away from the sore and it was the safest place to be right now.

# CHAPTER 11

**'OKAY EVERYONE, GATHER** round please.'

Thirty recruits assembled around me, eager to learn with notebooks in their hands and dressed in their army greens.

'Allow me to introduce myself. My name is Sergeant Jacob Turner, and I will teach basic field medicine. Now, today I am going to show you how to dress a bullet wound until help arrives.' Everyone stood around as the fake dummy began to bleed out, with coloured dye leaking out on the bed. The microphone repeated, *Help me! Help me!*

'Now you will notice that when I flip the dummy over, there is a hole in the back and blood is coming out, which indicates that the bullet has passed through, which is a good thing.'

The students were scared out of their minds. By the look of them, none of them had ever seen combat, let alone a dying person.

'First thing you do is clean the wound and place a patch on both sides. It is essential to move them as little as possible to prevent them from bleeding out. Also, it best to get help in five minutes to prevent the patient from bleeding out.' I had so much to teach this class, but as I looked at my watch, I realised

I had run out of time. 'Man, that two hours went by like nothing. Recruits, you know what you need to study and be prepared as we address burns; thank you all, you are dismissed!' It was funny watching the students all march out of the room like sheep; it took me back to my time in basic training.

My new role suited me. I was now a soldier and part-time medical instructor. Mackenzie felt that due to my combat experience, I would be more of an asset by teaching than being on the front lines.

I was now wearing the green uniform but I had a red cross around my biceps. On my shoulder, I had a staff sergeant insignia. Despite my disputes with Mackenzie, I kept the beard, but I did shave my head with a buzz cut. Anyway, now that class was finished, I went to find the girls. As I marched down that corridor, I had to admit it was great being in a position of power again, as every recruit I passed saluted me; it gave me just déjà vu, even back to the time when I was a staff sergeant. Over my time I think I must have trained over 300 soldiers. But the sad reality is that out of those 300, only 50 of them returned home, as the rest died overseas.

I checked out our private barracks, but all three of the bunks were empty, which is bizarre as this is where Tilley spent most of her time, reading and studying through her smart tablet. I eventually found her at the shooting range with one of the female instructors.

'Excellent form, Tilley! You're a natural shooter.'

Seeing Tilley in army camo gear and holding a rifle made me snap for some reason; imagining someone as innocent as Tilley as a soldier made me so angry. I stormed over to the shooting range while the instructor was teaching a class of 50 how to use a rifle.

'What the hell do you think you are doing!'

'Excuse me, Sergeant, I am teaching a class!"

'I don't care what you are doing! Why is Tilley a part of your class?'

'It is mandatory for everyone staying here to be conscripted to fight for the cause, so she is taking basic training just like the rest of us!'

'But she is ten years old! This is rubbish. I didn't sign up for this.'

The poor instructor was mortified that I was screaming at her, and her face was red. 'Listen, you!'

'Hey, hey, hey, what is going on?' Mackenzie appeared and stepped in to break us up.

'This lunatic is interrupting my class!'

The students all looked at me with shock. I could tell that Tilley was absolutely embarrassed.

'Jacob, a word ...' Mackenzie pulled me back and threw me into the barracks. 'What was that, Jacob?'

'I couldn't believe you put Tilley through that course, Mackenzie. She is just a child.'

'So were we, but we all have to learn. Why shouldn't she know how to fight?'

'Mackenzie, I have seen enough of my friends die. I don't want to lose another one, especially someone so young.'

'Jacob, you brought her into this mess when you picked her up. Look, Jacob, I get it, but you are not her father, and she needs to be able to handle herself. You can't protect her forever. Eventually, she must learn to care for herself. What has gotten into you? The old you never would have cared?'

I couldn't answer that question, and Mackenzie knew that, so she began walking out.

'Mackenzie, before you leave, I want you to know something ... some wisdom.'

'What's that?'

'What distinguishes us from the enemy is our morals. If we strip away those morals, then we are no different than the enemies we fight; remember that.'

Mackenzie was absolutely baffled by that comment and just left the room, forcing me to sigh. However, after thinking it over, I decided to apologise. But she was busy teaching how to shoot, so I held back and watched until she finished her class. I snucked behind a wall and ease dropped on their conversation:

*Bang! Bang!* as Tilley attempted to fire the sniper rifle at the target, Mackenzie fired a shot directly near her face, causing her to hit the ground and forcing her to laugh at the shock and loss of concentration.

'You flinched! A good sniper is willing to concentrate and focus no matter what the enemy throws at them. If they get distracted, they have lost the shot. So, focus!'

took a deep breath, placed her eye on the scope, breathed in … *Bang!* Mackenzie fired a shot next to her head.  panicked and pulled the trigger, and the bullet went flying, missing the marker. 'I am so bad. I wasn't cut out to be a sniper.'

'It takes time to develop that concentration and focus, but once you develop it, you never lose it.'

Suddenly sirens were heard throughout the bunker. 'Attention! Attention! Everyone needs to report to deck! Attention!' The place turned into a panic as soldiers rushed to make their way to the main deck, ready to receive orders.

'Jacob!' Mackenzie and  turned and saw me, not impressed that I was watching and listening.

'Mackenzie, I swear I—'

'No time! We need to go to the Command Centre. The commander will have more details.'

'Where's Tilley?'

'No time! The mission comes first.'

I nodded, and we all headed towards the Command Centre. As we entered, we felt a sense of urgency; the commander stood in the centre of the room, overseeing everything on the monitor. Everyone rushed by and scrolled through, gathering as much intel as possible.

Mackenzie approached. 'We are here, Commander. What do you need?'

'Excellent, Mackenzie. , Jacob, come along!

The commander escorted us to a table, and we all sat around with some of the commander's generals.

'Okay everyone, listen up. The annual military parade is coming up, and we have intel that the president himself will be attending in an open-limousine for the public to see.'

'Security is going to be tight, but if we strike at the right place, we may be able to take him down.'

'Mackenzie, you're the best sniper we have, so I will need you to take the shot … Alright? Meanwhile, Jacob, you are going to lead the troops on the ground. We need coordination as much as possible.'

'It's not going to be easy as the full force of the Asian Division's army will be on display. But I believe today we have found the kink in the dragon's armour, and we need to take it. Alright, everyone knows what they are doing, so Operation Abdicate is a go!'

After the debrief, we all got up from our table and headed to the hangar where we gathered our equipment. I only needed a change of clothing. After a few minutes of waiting around, I got in the Humvee and rolled out onto the main streets of Asian Division City.

We pulled up near an alley, and four other guys and I hopped out of the car. A crowd gathered in the street waiting for the military to march on through, separated by red valet lines stretching from the border wall to the fortified building known as the Great Hall of the People, where the president remained. We made sure we blended in as much as we could in the crowd. The only equipment I carried was an earpiece that allowed me to communicate with Mackenzie.

'Nightlife, this is Moses. Over!'

'What is your status, Moses?'

'I am—-oww!' I felt something hit the back of my neck. I reached back with my finger and felt blood. I turned around and looked everywhere, but I couldn't see anything.' *Where did it come from?*

'Moses, do you copy? Over.'

'I am fine, Nightlife. Am I in position? Over.'

'Roger, I am centred on a rooftop five nano-clicks away!'

'Roger that, scoping out the target.'

Security was beefing up as police dressed in heavy tactical gear guarded the street, waiting for the president to arrive. Then it began; the drums began to roll, and the bands came marching up the empty streets. Marching in unison, and goosestepping with such coordination that you couldn't even tell if they were human, the first wave of soldiers came marching down the road – thousands of them in clean, heavily armed uniforms keeping their rifles close to their chests as the crowd roared and applauded.

'Moses, Intel tells us that the president will be in the middle of the parade, about three units away!'

'Nightlife, are you ready to take the shot?'

'As ready as we will ever be. Spot out for snipers.'

I pulled out some binoculars from my back pocket and scanned around the rooftops looking for snipers.

'Okay, we have three snipers on three different rooftops, and there have to be thousands of police officers around here, so you need to be quick.'

Next came over one hundred tanks and thousands of artillery and missile launchers. The scariest thing was they had the capability to reach American Division City. Above, drones and small fighter planes circled overhead, and the more oversized bombers and aircraft flew over the drone in the Wastelands. I was impressed at the display of force. How America still outnumbers and outguns them is unbelievable.

'Jacob, be ready! The president is coming in his HongQi N701, so be ready.'

The second wave was coming in as thousands of troops and equipment rolled down the road. I could see the target over the horizon, and here he came, standing up in his limousine, giving out the royal wave. The president was well guarded, and dozens of police officers were trailing by his side as his car drove slowly so he could wave to the crowd. Luckily, there were so many people that nobody could spot me. Everyone was cheering, and I must admit that seeing him in real life was incredible as I had only seen him on international news outlets. But as his limousine drove past, I had an episode as the president turned to me and laughed sinisterly. His eyes briefly turned red, then I snapped out of it, and he returned to waving.

'Mackenzie, there are too many forces. Fall back!'

'Jacob, we need—' *Bang!* That was a sniper shot, but it didn't come from Mackenzie's direction; it came from the opposite direction as the crowd panicked and the police circled around the limousine with the president ducking inside and the hood of the heavily armoured limousine closed up.

'Blast, we have been compromised!' I used my binoculars. I looked over at where the shot came from and saw police snipers on the rooftop opposite Mackenzie. 'Mackenzie, are you there? Mackenzie!'

'Jacob, I've been hit—'

There was static coming from the other end, so I couldn't make out what she was saying.'

'Mackenzie! Mackenzie!'

Thank goodness for the group of people surrounding us, or else I would been shot by now, and just like that, I slipped back through the shadows and back into the alleyways. 'Command, this is Moses. This mission has been an absolute failure. Mackenzie is down … I repeat, Mackenzie is down!'

'I wouldn't say that!'

'Mackenzie, thank goodness you're alright.'

'I am not alright … I've been hit!'

'Roger that … are you safe?'

'Yes, the sniper's shot only grazed me, and I have managed to make it to the evacuation point.'

Wait, something is wrong. Why would Security and the police just let her go? I needed to get to the security point. But still, something about this didn't make sense. 'Coming to pick you up now. Making my way to the location now. I'm sorry to say this mission failed. We failed to kill the president.'

What's going on? There were cameras around the area; how have they not captured us yet? I didn't like this. Nevertheless, I managed to make it back to the Humvee and found Mackenzie nursing her shoulder. 'Here, give me a look at that shoulder.'

'Jacob, it's fine, it just grazed my shoulder.'

She was right, but that concerned me more as they had a clear shot at her, yet they missed her. How? The rest of the squad pulled up, and we all drove out of there, blending in with the other Humvee making its way from the failed military parade. There were sirens and police and army personnel rushing everywhere, yet not one of them batted an eye towards our Humvee, disappearing back to base.

We pulled up back at the base, but *agh!* The wound on the back of my neck began to cause sharp pain. 'Agh!' This time, a little louder.

'Jacob, are you alright?'

'Yer, just got a sore neck.'

Mackenzie smiled. 'Funny, I thought I was the one who got shot!'

'Yer, I know. Are you feeling alright?'

She just shrugged. 'Nothing I haven't had to endure before, but telling Command we failed the mission isn't going to be fun.'

The Commander stood in the Command Centre talking to and the other officials before turning to us. I couldn't tell if he was angry with us or if he was disappointed. We both stood at attention. Mackenzie began, 'Commander, we—'

He gestured for her to stop. 'Well done, Sergeant! This mission was an absolute success!'

Mackenzie and I were shocked. 'Sir, we failed to take out the president!'

'We never had a chance of taking out the president.' He clicked on the screen and showed blueprints from underneath the Great Hall of the People. 'No, our main goal was to locate the military compound underneath the Great Hall; that was the true intention of our mission.'

'You two were mainly the distraction, which I am happy to say Special Forces have happily retrieved the secret intel. Also, forces hit the fortified fortress when it was weakest, grabbing secret intel. So well done! We completed the mission.'

'Sir, what was on the intel!'

"I am afraid that is classified. Go, both of you. Get some rest and tend to that wound; you are both dismissed; we saluted and left as the Commander returned to view the monitor.

'Yes, Commander,' I whispered with a hint of bitterness, which Mackenzie picked up on. I stormed into the barracks where and Tilley sat playing board games. I was furious that they used us like pawns in their chess game. We were more valuable than that.

Mackenzie stormed in after me. 'Jacob, what the hell is your problem?'

'What's my problem? They used us as cannon fodder while they pulled some elaborate plan, and for what? I am sick to death of these organisations using suckers like us to fulfil their own agenda.'

'Suckers like us? Jacob, ever since you got here, you have looked down at us, questioning our actions and motives!'

'Mackenzie, I have been involved in movements like these before, and I can tell you there is nothing pure or righteous about them.'

'We are bringing freedom to China!'

'That's what the Chinese say!'

'Jacob, you've got the luxury of going home; the battle never stops ... you ran like a coward while people like me continued the fight.'

I shook my head. 'Some fights are not worth the loss.'

Mackenzie's face was red.

'I need to go for a walk.'

'Good. Go! And Jacob, you need to decide if you are with or against us.' Mackenzie turned around and pointed at and Tilley. 'And that goes for the rest of you too ... are you on board or not?'

At that point, I stormed out, slamming the door behind me. What is Mackenzie doing? Why is she aligning with these people? I needed to chill out; I needed to decide who I am. Am I a soldier, a wanderer or a freedom fighter? But as I was walking down the corridor, I quickly turned around and noticed it!

The laughter ... the laughter in my mind as if my own brain was turning against me. Am I that much of a lunatic that even my own mind judges me? It's funny that I thought I was free, but sometimes I feel as if the only proper way to be free is to die. Sometimes I think about what would have happened if I had died in that helicopter. A chill ran down my spine, and I had the strange urge to go to the Command Room; a normal, rational person would just ignore it. But I needed closure as to why my mind was dragging me there. I peered around a corner and noticed two security guards with their rifles close to their chests, like toy soldiers.

Great! How was I going to get past them! Suddenly, I turned around and they had disappeared, as if they were never there! A trick from a sick brain, then I heard him say, 'Walk. Jacob, walk!'

I stood and began walking towards the sliding door as the door shot bac. 'Good Jacob, good, Now walk!' I entered the Command Room and men in suits looked at me.

'Jacob, you can't be here!' The commander approached me and said, 'Jacob, I am giving you a direct order! What are you doing here? Return to your barracks now!'

I was shocked that I had entered the room. *Ask him Jacob. Ask him the question.* 'What question?' I accidentally said out loud, which caused the commander to give me a weird look.

'Jacob, what are you talking about?'

*Ask him, Jacob. You know, deep down, the question. Ask him!*

I stopped listening to what my mind and heart had to say; it finally hit me, so I looked up and stared at the commander, which creeped him out. 'Commander, how long will you keep lying to us?'

Everyone in the Command Room stopped what they were doing and looked at me.

'Stop lying! You say you're here to liberate Asian Division City, then why have you got factions spread across the globe?'

'To spread our message across the globe and to gather resources and information we need to take down the city. See, here is the funny thing about freedom … there is no such thing as true freedom unless you replace it with something powerful.'

'So, what do you plan to replace Asian Division City with once you overthrow the government?'

The commander seemed confused as to what I was saying. Hell, even I was confused about what was happening. The door opened and I rushed towards the commander's office.

'Someone stop that man!' Security guards came rushing towards me. But I quickly made it into the office and sealed the door; there were rapid bangs at the door. I had to hurry. Wasting no time, I opened the commander's computer; by now, all the files would have been transferred digitally. But I still faced a big problem: how was I supposed to unlock the commander's computer?

*Okay, come on Jacob! Come on Jacob! Use your brain. What could the password be?*

I didn't know what I was doing, but I knew I was running out of time as I could hear the cutting tools slowly cutting through the door. I opened my eyes and was successful! The computer was unlocked, and I started searching. Wait! Was that nuclear weapon blueprints? But I thought that after the nuclear war, and the capability to build nuclear weapons was diminished. The commander was planning on building tactical nuclear weapons! But why? I kept digging, and after searching through the documents, I found … oh my! Then, Security broke through the door, and it exploded into multiple pieces. Two soldiers pinned me to a desk, and two more entered the room and stood next to the commander as he stood over me.

I screamed at him. 'You bastard! This isn't just about Asian Division City; you are planning a global coupe! A new one-world government!'

The commander just smiled. 'A new world order! With me as Supreme Leader! Alright, that's enough! Take him away.'

As the soldier dragged me out of the office and out the door, I watched as the commander went back to watching the monitor and looking at his tablet. I screamed, 'You fool! You're going to drive the world into a war!'

The commander looked at me one more time and said calmly, '*There is a time for peace and a time for war ...*'

# CHAPTER 12

**I WAS THROWN** across my cell with such force that I fell to the ground and laid there in the dark for hours on end, with no food or light. What was only an hour felt like an eternity; then, without warning, two guards entered the room and pulled me up, .

The commander appeared. 'How did you know?'

'Know what?'

'The nuclear weapons – how did you know?'

'I suggest you listen to him, Jacob.' Mackenzie stood next to him wearing a white tank top and army camo pants.

'Mackenzie, I can explain.'

'No need to explain! How could you betray us? Betray me!'

The commander held her shoulder. 'Jacob here is a heretic; he doesn't see our vision. In truth, he is a stupid brute. But no need to fear, together we will create a new world in our vision, free of corruption and injustice.'

I smirked. 'So you are a god now?'

The commander snapped his fingers and the guard to my right whacked me on the back of my head, which caused me to fall to the ground.

'Mackenzie, please! His intentions are not pure; he is only trying to seek power for himself. He is just as evil as the tyrant he is attempting to overthrow, and he has plans to build nuclear weapons. Ask! Ask what he plans to use the weapons for.'

Mackenzie paused, trying to think of what to do next. 'What are the nuclear weapons for?'

'He is planning to use them in any city that does not support him or his views, and he is planning to use them in all of them, including our home!'

She turned to the commander, wanting answers. 'Is that true?'

'Mackenzie, I wish it wasn't true, but it is. Do you remember what happened to the world when China and America were in control? It's simple ... they destroyed each other and took the world with them. If this world is to be rebuilt, it needs a new power! And I—' The commander stopped, as we could all hear a ticking noise. 'Everyone be quiet! What is that noise?'

The commander heard it coming from me and walked towards me. He looked at my neck and saw the red glow. 'Jacob, you idiot!'

*Bang!* Everyone turned around to hear gunfire echoing from outside the cell and the bunker glowing red from sirens and red lights.

'Jacob, what have you done?'

The pain in my neck was a tracker; they had been tailing us the entire time, and now the Chinese government had closed in on us. The commander and Mackenzie quickly fled the room. Using the chaos, I took out the guards and made my way out of the cell. Now to find Ashilya and Tilley and get the hell out of here!

The gunfire echoing through the hall and down to the floor below was really messing with my already diseased mind. I could feel that my mind was caught between the battle of old and the current battle I was in, and with everything going on with the Vendor, I didn't know what was reality.

Soldiers passed me by, rushing back and forth with rifles, only to never be seen again, cut down in the thick of the battle. Luckily for me, they'd locked me deep within the heart of the bunker, so the battle hadn't reached me yet. But I was scared, scared of losing Ashilya and Tilley. I had to find them quickly, or else they would likely be another casualty. As I climbed up, the noises increased until I reached the final hanger, and it was absolute hell! There was fire everywhere; the entire place was covered in destroyed military equipment, and there was a constant barrage of bolt and bullet fire covering the sky. On one side were the defenders, the Republic forces, and on the other side, the Communist army. However, the Asian Division Army had overwhelming manpower and military equipment heading their way, and within five hours, this entire bunker would be overrun.

In the thick of the battle, I was caught completely off-guard when I saw ten-year-old Tilley mounted on a machine gun firing towards the enemy.

'Tilley, come on, we need to leave.'

'No, Jacob! The battle is not over'

'Yes, it is Tilley, now run!'

She stopped firing and looked up at me as we tried our best to dodge the bullets. I could see she was beginning to cry. 'Jacob, I don't want to die!'

I whispered in her ear. 'Tilley, on the count of three, let go and run … Are you ready? One, two, three! RUN!'

Tilley jumped off the machine gun. I took over as Tilley ran, crying at the sound of every bullet flying past her, while I opened fire at the Chinese soliders. Luckily for both of us, we were in a bad position and could barely hit anything. This gun was outdated; it bounced off the soldiers' modern body armour.

After Tilley was out of the way, I abandoned my position and ran to our barracks. If there was any chance of finding the girls, it was there, and I was right. I entered the barracks and found  hugging Tilley, who, after seeing me, ran over and hugged me.

'Come on, girls, let's get out of here!'

*Bang!* I turned around. Mackenzie was blocking our escape holding a laser pistol. 'I am sorry, Jacob, I can't let you go!' She shot a bolt that missed my head and hit the back wall.

'You missed ... you never miss.'

'It was a warning. I am sorry, Jacob, but I have orders.'

'To hell with your orders ... please, Mackenzie, if there is anything good left inside you, you will abandon your orders and come with us.'

Mackenzie just shook her head and began to cry. 'I can, Jacob ... but you promised me all those years ago that we were going to go home together.'

'Yes, I remember.'

'So why did you abandon me?'

'I'm sorry, Mackenzie, I left you alone; I was following orders.'

'So am I.' She looked confused.

'Jacob, they tortured me, they beat me, and they did unspeakable things to me, and where were you?'

'I ran Mackenzie, but I always looked back at that moment, and it still haunts me to this day, and I know that for you, the battle is never over. But please don't do this; let's end this fight together. Please, this is not your fight.'

She frowned for a minute, contemplating the offer, and then her face quickly focused as she shot at the door behind us, which forced it to shut down and seal off the soldiers behind us.

'There is an old abandoned tunnel system. I think you have seen it before.'

I nodded. 'Yes, the tunnel with the vines.'

'That will lead you out into the docks. Take it and go! I will meet you there!'

'Thank you, Mackenzie.' I quickly grabbed the girls' hands and escorted them out the door. 'Hey, Mackenzie!'

She turned around to face me.

'On the street where I live, there is this nightclub that is located downstairs; when we get out of this, the first round is on me.'

Mackenzie just smiled. 'I would love that, but no time to talk. Go!'

As the girls and I descended back down into the bunker, Mackenzie disappeared out of view and the gunshots grew quiet. We finally reached the old abandoned tunnel covered in vines; the only reason I remembered this place was that the commander showed me it as it was his favourite place to go. It was completely void of light of any kind, and I couldn't see the other side, so it was like walking into a mineshaft. We didn't know where we were going or if there was an exit, but we had to have faith that it would lead us to where we needed to go.

# CHAPTER 15

**TILLEY AND I** entered the tunnel and it gradually got so dark that I could barely see my hands. Luckily, I had  and Tilley to keep me company; however, after a while, I turned around and they were gone!

'! Tilley! Where are you!?'

'Hello?' The voice was female. In a desperate attempt, I made my way towards the voice as it was calling me again. 'Hello?' But the voice now sounded like a that of a young man; In fact, it sounded like my voice. Then, out of the darkness, I saw some light like that of a porch light. As I got closer to it, I saw an old red wooden door similar to the front of my house. I stumbled closer and closer and reached for the doorknob—I was back in the living room of my destroyed family house in American Division City; however, it was much cleaner and more modern. In the living room sat two children: a young version of me dressed in pyjamas, and next to me was my ten-year-old sister, Remy, who was also dressed in her pyjamas. We were playing a board game. Remy was my older sister, a beautiful girl who took after Anna, with black hair and hazel eyes. Anna was in the kitchen cooking us a lovely roast and preparing dinner. Suddenly, our dad came bursting through the front door of the house, drunk out of his mind.

'Bill, where have you been?'

'Get off my ass, I am trying to find employment.'

'Really? Because it looks like you are half-drunk again!'

'Don't start with me, Anna, I am doing the best I can to help keep a roof over our head.'

Remy and I continued playing our board game, trying our best to escape the reality of the monster abusing our mother. Our father was a flawed man; he had struggled with drug and alcohol addiction, and the sad fact was that he would take it out on us, in particular our mother. Anna and Bill were going at it, screaming back and forth until *whack!* He struck my mother across the face with enough force to force her on the ground. Remy and I just stood there in shock as our father galloped up the stairs to collapse in our bathroom. Mum just laid there and cried as we both rushed over to hug her.  The current me watched the suppressed memory from years past, and I could see the younger version of myself staring directly at me, peeling back the veil of time as if my inner child was trying to tell me something. My younger version broke away from my mother and rushed up the stairs. As I slowly walked up the stairs, the environment around me changed. I was now in my room; this time, it was a fourteen-year-old pimply version of myself in a high-school blazer sitting next to the open window and blowing cigarette smoke out the window. I started smoking and drinking at a very young age as it helped me to cope with the abuse and trauma, nursing the bruises and black eyes that my father left on me. After finishing the smoke, I threw the butt out the window and called for his sister.

'Remy ... Hey Remy!' I knocked on her door then entered, without waiting for her to invite me in. 'Hey Remy, Mum wants us to—' My adolescent sister stood at the end of her bed with a packed suitcase. Her room was empty.

'Remy, what is this?'

'Jacob, I am sorry, but I can't do this anymore!'

'What do you mean?'

Remy was trying to maintain her strength, but she crumbled and began to cry. 'Jacob, I can't take the trauma and the abuse, watching my family members being hurt and the years of screaming!'

I was utterly shocked; the only source of strength was leaving me: 'What about Mum?'

'What about her? Jacob, I'm sorry, but I need to get out of here. Mum is a resilient woman. She can survive without me.'

I just looked down, sad that my big sister was leaving; teenage Jacob began crying as I just watched. It was like watching a movie of myself, having to relive this ordeal. Remy rushed up and hugged me. 'Come here, little bro.'

'I can't believe you are leaving me.'

'I will come back for you, I promise.' My sister finished packing, picked up her suitcase, and began walking down the staircase. But she broke down as she was about to walk out the door. 'I can't, I can't do it!'

Young me rushed towards her. 'Hey listen, I think you should go; you deserve better … I can take care of Mum. You go save yourself.'

She turned to me. 'What about you?'

'I can take care of Mum, you go!'

Remy hugged me, 'Love you, Jacob.'

'Love you, sis.'

We exchanged one last hug, and she opened the door and disappeared out of my life – I never saw her again. My teenage version just stood at the door with a feeling of loneliness overwhelming him. But then, out of the blue, he rushed out the door, which wasn't part of the memory, and I followed after him.

This time, it was a sixteen-year-old version of myself standing at the end of a military barracks, lined up with other children dressed in army camos with buzzcuts and white singlets, as a man dressed as the staff sergeant came walking down the halls. 'Alright you sorry excuse for maggots, you have to be the worse excuse for cadets I have ever seen. I bet none of you will even make it past training.' Then the trainer stopped and looked at my younger version. 'What's your name, Private?'

'Sir, my name is Jacob!'

'Can you swim, Jacob?'

'I have never been near water, sir.'

'Never been near water and you want to join the navy? Private, you must be the stupidest cadet I have ever trained. I am going to call you Moses. I hope you like boats because the day that I let you become a radiation diver is the day I become the king of America! Now get down and give me ten push-ups ... now maggot!'

I watched my adolescent version drop on the floor and struggle to give ten push-ups as the staff sergeant walked up the corridor and disappeared.

This time, the memory changed, and I saw myself in a military uniform sitting near the Shanghai docks. I was dressed in a dirty, torn navy-seal uniform, smoking a cigarette.

An officer rushed over to me. 'Sergeant Turner, take that cigarette out of your mouth and get a move on!'

It was evacuation day, the worst day in American Division history. We lost the offensive of Asian Division City and were pushed back to the dock. Thousands of troops rushed to evacuate equipment as ships returned to American Division City, while overheard turrets rushed to cut down enemy fighter jets and bombers. The general leading the mission stood up and faced thousands of people: 'Everyone! Get on the ships now!'

Like rats, everyone scrambled in a panic as the forces drew close to our location, but I was looking for someone, asking random people, 'Excuse me, has anyone seen Mackenzie?'

Someone yelled out, 'Jacob, Mackenzie didn't make it. She died.'

Hearing that, my heart sank; Mackenzie was like a sister to me; hell, I knew her longer than my sister. In a brief moment, I broke down on the docks, crying as everyone rushed around me; the pain was so intense that I could barely move.

'Jacob, Get up!'

I looked up, and it was my old staff sergeant from years back. He had climbed the ranks and had a few more grey hairs than I remembered, but nonetheless, here he was. 'Sir, I can't … I can't keep moving on; it's too hard.'

'Jacob, you sorry waste of skin, get up now! You can't go down because the pain is too great. Get up! Get up now! Get Up!'

Younger me screamed, but I was able to get back on my feet, and we walked up the ramp together and watched as we hit the open sea. The last thing I saw was a destroyed enemy fighter jet come crashing down into the ocean, and I watched as one memory transitioned to another; now it was me from a couple months ago. I was in the same room back in my family house, except now it was a bit more worn out as I stared out the window, smoking a cigarette and drinking bourbon, looking out at the streets, taking in the night sky. Then I heard a banging at the door!

'I'm just in here, Mum!' But I was wrong, as Edward walked into the room, my long-deceased best friend.

'Well, I don't know about you, but I do look good in a dress.'

I couldn't help giggling and went back to staring out the window. Edward jumped on my bed and poured himself a bourbon. There was silence.

'Edward, do you ever think about your life?'

He looked shocked. 'Where did that come from?'

'I've just been thinking about life and how painful it has been.'

'Come on, Jacob, don't think of life like that; life is what you make of it. Take my life, for example, I went from a wealthy household to broke-back poor.'

'And would you say you are happy.'

'Well, I am not unhappy.'

'I don't know, Edward, I am just tired.'

'Oh Jacob, you big softie … Look! I get with everything going on with your mum and work, but we just got to keep getting out of bed in the morning and doing our best.'

I smirked and looked down at my drink. 'You're right, Edward. Thank you. You're a good friend.'

He placed a hand on my back and looked out the window with me, each of us with a drink in our hands. 'It's you and me against the world.'

My current self watched on joyfully; it was one of my favourite memories … then I heard my name being called out again.

'Jacob!' The voice sounded familiar. I snapped back to reality and found  and Tilley standing right next to me. I had completely lost track of time. We were near the end of the tunnel, and it led to a drain outside the Shanghai dock. We had made it, but the commander was pointing a handgun at us with his suit torn, and a large scar across his face. He looked worn out and weak. Influential people can end up broken people just like the rest of us if their aura and authority is taken away, and they turn out to be weaker. But right now, he had a gun, so we had to play along.

'Jacob, you and your team ruined everything. You brought my father's army on me and ruined my entire operation!'

I just stood there with my hands in the air. 'Let's just cut the bullshit. You never cared about your people; you just wanted to get back at your father. You're just like him ... a warlord who profits off the backs of others.'

'I am nothing like my father! My father never made time for me; he was always busy with political affairs and overseas trips.'

'You entitled little brat. Daddy didn't show you enough love, so you think you can just burn the world down and hurt people as you please!'

'Shut up!' He turned the gun and pointed it directly at me.

'Let me ask you a question before you shoot me. Was that restaurant story real?'

'It was, and it taught me an important lesson: society moves fast; no one cares about tradition or the past. No! Relevancy is built around the power to manipulate society – a power I thought I could tame. Oh well, I guess I will have to take it out on you.'

I stretched out my arm to protect  and Tilley as they huddled behind me. *Bang! Bang! Bang!*

The commander looked down to find three bullet holes in his chest, which were all leaking blood into his white shirt. His face went white, and he collapsed to the floor. Behind him was a bruised Mackenzie holding a pistol.

'Mackenzie, thank goodness.' But as I was about to walk over to her and give her a hug, she turned the pistol to face me. 'Mackenzie, look, I am sorry—'

'Turn around!'

I choked a little, looking at the stern expression on her face. So, I turned my back on her, thinking she was going to shoot me.

Suddenly I felt an electric bolt hit me in the back, forcing me to collapse to the floor. The bolt blasted my nerves, causing my pain receptors to scream in agony, and I began to cry and breathe heavily.

'Oh, suck it up, Jacob, it's a stun bolt. You will be fine in a couple of minutes. I just needed to shoot you to disable the tracker in the back of your neck ... Are you alright?'

The pain gradually wore off, and I was able to get back to my fee. 'Fine! Awesome ... now that we have escaped, we must get to the docks!'

'Why?'

'To get to American Division City.'

'I am sorry, Jacob. I'm not coming back.'

'What?'

'I still have work to do.'

'Jacob, there are cells all across the world, and with them, we can do good; yes, we were led with a tyrant, but under new leadership, we can change the world.'

'I wish you well, Mackenzie; they are in good hands. Alright, , Tilley, we have to make our way to the docks.' I was excited we were finally going home; I couldn't wait to show and Tilley America. 'Man, I can't wait for the two of—'

I looked back. I was thinking so far ahead that I didn't realise  and Tilley hadn't moved an inch. They stood there looking at me.

', Tilley, is everything okay?'

 looked at me sadly. 'I'm sorry, Jacob, I'm not coming.'

'But you always wanted to come to America.'

'I know, but my village needs me more! Jacob, I have been talking with Mackenzie, and if I work with her, I could finally help to liberate my village.'

I had to admit I was disappointed, but I understood completely. 'Alright then, I will take Tilley, and you can meet us in America. Come on, Tilley!' But I looked over, and Tilley hadn't moved an inch.

I shook my head. 'No way! No way am I going to let you recruit a kid. No way!'

'Jacob—'

Tilley stopped  from finishing her sentence and she walked over to me. 'Jacob, thank you for protecting me, but I need to be with them. They are my family and they need me. Please let me be with them.'

I sighed. Tilley was the last person I wanted to let go, but I was not her dad, and she needed people to be with her. 'Okay, kid, just know if you need anything at all, I will be there in a heartbeat.'

Tilley ran up and hugged me, and  did the same. We all hugged for a couple of minutes before the two girls walked over to Mackenzie and began holding hands as they headed back into the tunnel, slowly disappearing into the darkness.

'Mackenzie, wait!'

All three turned around to face me.

'I will keep that beer nice and cold for you.'

'I would like that, Jacob, I would like that!'

They turned back into the tunnel and disappeared. For them, their battle wasn't over. I was left out in the bright light as the sun shone on the back of my head. I guess this was the part of my personal journey where I had to walk alone. All I could do was walk away from the tunnel.

# CHAPTER 16

**WHERE TO GO** from here? While being free was great, I needed to find a way home. But first, I had to find something that would allow me to survive the radiation. Then, in front of me, I saw him – a random dock worker wearing a radiation suit … *Don't worry, I didn't kill him.* He is merely sleeping, but the poor guy probably needs to call in sick tomorrow. Okay, now that I had a radiation suit, I needed to find a shipping container that was going to take me home as I couldn't just walk onto a cargo ship as this dock was crawling with troops.

The Shanghai docks are considered one of the busiest container ports in the world. Every day, shipping containers come in containing hundreds of cargo containers from many different cities around the world. Around me were hundreds of shipping containers of various sizes as forklifts and dock workers worked around the clock to move the shipping containers into place. Ducking and weaving, I snuck around the containers, moving like a ninja on the rooftop. I walked and jumped around, hoping to find a container to get me home. *Come on! Come on!* There had to be a container that would get me home.

After searching for a long time, I found a red shipping container with the words *Wacco INC* written on it; I knew this company and knew it would take me home. So as the drone flew past, I quickly lifted the door open slowly enough to hide the noise from the drone, which did alert them for a split-second when the door slammed shut, leaving me in an empty shipping container in the dark. *Wait, empty?* Why was the container empty? Nonetheless, this was my ticket to get home, so I had to take it. I curled up in a ball as the outside started to rain acid, but that's alright. These containers are built to withstand the harsh environment outside and were even built to protect humans from the radiation. Yet it was eerily scary being in the dark as the mind began to play tricks on me; the silence was killing me. But it didn't matter as I was desperate to make it home.

'Ha-ha-ha-ha!'

I heard the laughter coming from outside the container.

'Oh no, it's you!'

'Oh Jacob, always on the run, always hiding like the rat you are.'

I stood up, looking around. 'Why don't you come and face me like a man?!'

Then, two long skeleton-like hands grabbed the container door as smoke began to form, and two giant red eyes emerged, staring directly at me. 'Okay, if you insist!'

Suddenly, the arms opened the door and disappeared. I walked over to the now-open hole to find that I was on the deck of a cargo ship in the middle of the rough ocean. Gigantic waves slammed against the ship's hull, making it rock side to side. It wasn't long before I could barely stand straight. Also, the occasional thunderclap in the sky lit the sky with blue flashes.

Then I heard him again: 'Welcome aboard, Jacob! You and I going to have some fun.'

'Where are you?'

'Come make your way to the captain's deck!'

I walked across the deck and slowly up the stairs, but what awaited me inside sickened me. I found the crew of four, including the captain, dead on the floor with their throats slit and blood covering their white uniform. The Vendor just laughed his sinister laugh, and thunder ripped through the sky. I looked at the captain's dead body as the Vendor's zombified face looked at me. His eyes glowed red. 'Welcome aboard the sinking ship ... ha-ha-ha!'

I couldn't look at his face so I rushed out of the captain's deck and onto the stairs.

'You're looking scared. Young Master Jacob wants to go home to his mummy.'

'What are you?'

'Depends on your perspective; to some, I am an angel, while to others, I am a devil.'

'Are you the Devil?'

'You can call me that, but I go by many names, such as Bogeyman. But the truth is, I am what remains in your mind.'

'Why are you doing this to me?'

'Simple ... you invited me in! You did this by feeding your head with pain and sorrow; I merely had to feed off it to exist.'

'Well, you failed, Tilley is safe.'

'Amazing. Someone with such vision and clarity is so blind. Tilley is merely a construct. Her existence matters not to me.'

'I saw your red eyes everywhere.'

'That is because I am everywhere. I am the voice in your head, in your holograms, in your music, in your politicians, in your news. I am in everyone, and this world is mine to bend and control. Now get to the lower deck of the ship. Better run, little Moses.'

I swung open the door to the lower deck, only to be met with a cold chill. All I could see was darkness, yet at the bottom of the stairs, I swear I could see a skeleton hand slowly scraping the right side of the wall before disappearing into the darkness. I had to remind myself not to be afraid;

I heard, 'What are you afraid of, Jacob?' as I slowly descended.

'You don't know anything about me, pal!'

'Oh, I know everything about you; I know your fears, your anxieties and the pain you hide deep within your innermost mind. I also know your deepest desire! By the way, did you end up sleeping with Ella?'

I continued to walk into the darkness, not knowing what to find: 'The tree, the tree that gave me my power, what is it?'

'Simple, just a tree; it was nothing special; it was just how you perceived it; it's me who gives you those powers; it's not some serum or magical tree. No! It is me, the power lives within me. I just don't know how to use it.'

I continued to walk, but as I made my way through the cargo cold, the voice of all my friends and family began speaking in my head: *Loser! Failure! Murderer! Liar! Monster!* Over and over again it played in my head until I collapsed onto the floor. 'Stop it!'

He only laughed. 'You are so weak; no wonder you lose everyone you get too close too.'

'What do you want?'

The ominous being then converted himself from spirit to flesh, taking the form of a pale white man with blonde hair and blue eyes, shirtless wearing only blue jeans. 'I want a rematch! Put them up.'

I got to my feet and placed myself into a fighting position. I swung at him, but none of the punches seemed to hit him, and when I went to hit him with a pipe near the floor, he merely laughed. Out of nowhere, he pushed his palm into my chest. As the kinetic energy surged through my body, I went flying into the air, but the being didn't want to kill me as I phased through the entire deck, I passed through them as if they were air. It was incredible, no pain ... as if I was a ghost landing on the deck of the ship, back out in the rain with the rough seas belting the side of the boat. The being then passed through the deck of the ship and stood right in front of me; I was defeated.

'What do you want?'

'You know what I want.' The figure reached into his pant pocket, conjured a Glock handgun, and threw it at my feet. 'I want you to use the weapon on yourself, end your life so we can escape this dreaded reality.'

I picked up the gun, looked at it.

'Come on, Jacob, do it! You know you want to. Ain't you tired of the pain and suffering? Come, Jacob, you are too weak to continue!'

But that comment struck me and brought me to my senses. I clenched my fist into a ball. 'No, I am not weak!'

The figure looked shocked as I got to my knees. 'You're right. I have been through pain; I have endured suffering. Hell, I even make mistakes that I am not proud of. But through it all, I know deep down I am a good man, and you know what? I forgive! I forgive myself, and I forgive everyone who hurt me.'

The being was shocked. 'You forgive?'

'Yes, I forgive!'

The Vendors face went red, and he let out an angry scream that generated two gigantic bat wings. He flew into the ocean. I heard a splash, and there was quiet. Suddenly, a gigantic being made of pure water emerged with two red eyes; his body was so transparent that I could see fish swimming around deep within it. He let out a gigantic roar. 'You little maggot, I can destroy you in a minute!'

I don't get it. The creature has all this power, so why couldn't he kill me himself. But then I realised he can't kill me; I mean, yes, he can hurt, but he can't kill me. Knowing this information, I stood tall in defiance. 'Do it!'

'What?'

'Destroy me! Go on, do it!'

He lifted his gigantic transparent, watery hand and was about to swing out. At that moment, I felt scared and flinched. Under my breath, I muttered the words, 'Father, forgive me!', as the figure's hand was about to strike me, but it flinched back in pain. I opened my eyes and realised that I wasn't hurt … I wasn't even wet. I could see it … a dome of pure light. I couldn't touch it, but it managed to protect me and hurt him as the figure nursed his hand then looked at me in anger, With his other hand, he tried to strike me again, only for the shield to protect me from harm. I could see the fear on the his face, so I began to walk up to him,

'You have no power over me. No matter what you are, I am not afraid, for I am saved!'

The Vendor looked shocked. 'You have the spirit!'

Suddenly, a bright white light appeared in the sky above the ship, and even he looked up. It was beautiful and warm, shining on me, and I could hear a sound; it sounded like the flapping of wings; it sounded like an angel. Was it God?

But once the light got closer, it turned out it was the spotlight on an HH-100G Pave Hawk. The helicopter flew above me as the mysterious Vendor disappeared into the night leaving no trace. Two ropes from the chopper were thrown down and two American Division navy seals slid down and attached a harness over me. 'It's okay, you are safe. We are going to get you out!'

I didn't know what to say as I was at a loss for words. After attaching the harness, they hoisted me up into the helicopter, and I was surrounded by four men.

'Thank you for saving me, but how did you know where I was?'

'We received a distress call from the captain. It's okay. Are you American?'

'Yes!'

'Great, let's get you home!'

Finally, I was heading home. 'Thank you … what's your names?'

The first one on my right spoke. 'My name is Gabriel. Joshua is behind me; the seal to your left is Rachel, and our pilot's name is Michael. Don't worry, you are safe!'

We all sat there in silence, staring out the helicopter window as a giant tidal wave came in and wiped the abandoned cargo ship into the sea, disappearing from sight. Our helicopter flew away to the nearest carrier.

# CHAPTER 17

**SO, THERE IS** good news, and there is bad news. The excellent news was that I was soon shipped back to American Division City after arriving on the American Division navy aircraft carrier. The bad news is I am not free. Unfortunately, the previous charges I had before leaving American Division City had not been resolved; added to that were charges for manslaughter, mass murder and piracy. So, I was given life in prison. I would have gotten the death sentence, but after being checked over by a psychiatrist, I was found to have schizophrenia and deemed legally insane. Apparently making up stories about creatures with wings and little girls in the forests didn't sit well with the authorities.

So, I am back in Quinnestial Prison in the white-padded cell, except this time there is no roommate; it was just me, myself, and I. On the bright side, the doctors are giving me anti-psychotic medication, so I will not be seeing the Vendor anytime soon, I hope. All I do is lie on my bunk, staring at the ceiling. I have to admit that it was lovely being back with no bills to pay, free meals, and no big adventure, just living the peaceful life of a prisoner. That was until a woman sporting a black suit and wearing glasses walked into my room.

'Jacob William Turner?'

'Yes, that is me. But I'm sure you know that already.'

She ignored my sarcasm. 'Agent Mirka, Secret Service.' She held up a holographic projector of her credentials, showing the Secret Service emblem on it with a photo of her face.

'What's up? Afraid I am going to kill the president or something? Even though I'm in prison?'

Again, she ignored my sarcasm. 'The president wants to speak to you personally.'

I looked at her, shocked. 'Really! President Hawkins wants to see me personally?'

'Former President Richard Hawkins was voted out of office just a couple of month ago; we have a new president!'

Make sense in the months that I was gone I had no form of communication with America and hadn't seen the news in months.

Great, another businessman in a suit. 'May I ask who it is?'

'The president knew of your lack of knowledge and requested I keep it a secret. But she requested I bring you to meet her.'

I got off my bunk and walked to the door. 'Alright, lead the way!'

We walked through the front door of the prison and stepped into a black limousine. A few moments later, we arrived at the Capital Autonomous Zone. Under the ParliaCongress building sat the Presidential Chamber, which was built underground in case of a nuclear attack.

After entering the building, I was escorted through various tunnels until we arrived at the president's office, which resembled the Oval Office from the former White House, complete with blue drapery, navy-blue rugs with the seal of the president on them, blue wallpaper, cream-coloured sofas, a fake window with a phony display of America Division City, and of course, near the window sat the *Resolute* Desk, where the newly elected president was sitting on her chair buried deep in paperwork and signing bills, too busy to notice us. She wore a blue dress and white pearls adorned her neck. Her hair was black and she had blue eyes. She was thin and looked to be in her 30s.

The Secret Service agent knocked on the door. 'Madam President, your guest has arrived.'

'Wonderful. You may leave us.'

'Madam, given everything …'

The president raised a hand, and the Secret Service agent stopped talking.

'I can handle this; I have known him for a long time.'

I stared as Agent Mirka bowed and left the room, closing the door behind her. The new president placed her pen on the table, leaned back on her chair, faced me, and smiled at my presence.

'It's been a very long time, Jacob!'

'Sis, is it really you?!'

# EPILOGUE

**IN THE DOME** city of Kabul, the president of the Afghan regime, Ghayr Muhimin, was sitting on his throne, a 40-year-old man with a black-and-grey beard wearing a black turban and a Pirhan Tumban. To the left and right of him stood two royal guards in their bright-green uniforms holding plasma rifles.

A voice came through the holographic projector. 'Sir, we have the wife selection now!'

'Send them in.'

The golden palace door opened and three women, fully clothed in burkas and robes, entered. They were forced to kneel before the president as he got up from his throne and slowly descended the stairs.

'Look at this lovely line up,' he said as he rubbed his hand across their burqa.

The first woman had blue eyes, and the second one had brown eyes. But the third woman had a brown left eye and her right eye was white, which caught the president's attention.

'This one interests me; bring her before the throne.'

As the two royal guards lifted her up and brought her before the throne, the president sat back down. The guard quickly removed her burqa to reveal a young woman with black hair.

'What is your name?'The woman looked up at him and mumbled, 'My name is Yasmin.'

'That's a beautiful name … now you will be one of my wives. But first, I must check you. Remove her clothes!'

As the guards began to rip off her robes there was a loud noise and a red bolt flew into the throne room, taking out the royal guard on the right. A second bolt took out the guard on the left, who fell to the ground. The president began to panic and reached for his holographic projector. However, before he could signal for help, Yasmin lunged at him and stabbed him in the neck. As the president sat on his throne, gripping his neck, blood rushed, and he collapsed on the floor door, dead.

Yasmin clicked her eye. 'Mama Bird, this is Desert Fox; the president is down.'

Crouched on the rooftop above the president's temple was covered in a burqa and holding a laser sniper rifle, which she had used to take out the royal guards.

'Roger that, Sis … Nightlife, did you get that?'

In a command centre, Mackenzie stared at the monitor. She had taken over the operation, but this time under new leadership. She wore a smart suit and the United Nations flag hung above her.

'Alright girls, extracting you now!' Mackenzie looked at a giant world map on the monitor.